DISCARD

JONAH SEES GHOSTS

by Mark J. Sullivan, III

Published by Akashic Books
©2003 Mark J. Sullivan, III

ISBN: 1-888451-04-1
Library of Congress Control Number: 2002116773

Akashic Books
PO Box 1456
New York, NY 10009
Akashic7@aol.com
www.akashicbooks.com

JONAH SEES GHOSTS

by Mark J. Sullivan, III

AKASHIC BOOKS
New York

ACKNOWLEDGMENTS

Thanks to Johnny Temple, Johanna Ingalls, Jessie Hutcheson, Bill MacKaye, Jennifer Ballard, Gabrielle Danchick, Henry Rollins, Joseph Cummins, Sohrab Habibion, Michael Parillo, and Rick Farr.

For Elly, the love of my life

PRODIGAL DAD

DAN HART DIED ON HIS SON JONAH'S sixth birthday. Jonah waited quietly all day long for his father who, filled with several lunchtime martinis and fumbling with the tape deck, had run off the road and cut his throat on his way through the windshield. Hidden from sight in the gully where he had landed, he bled to death and waited three days for discovery.

*

After the call from the state trooper, Susan Hart replaced the receiver and began jotting notes for the funeral on a pad she kept by the phone. There was Mr. Stevenson at the funeral parlor. And Dan's parents. And the other partners at the firm. She sat down in the chair next to the phone table there in the front hallway and put the end of the pen in her mouth while she thought who else. She couldn't think of anyone.

*

Susan had known her husband was dead for about forty-eight hours now, the way you sometimes just know a thing. The difference between Susan and most people, though, was that when Susan just knew something, she acted upon the knowledge. Her self-confidence was such that, early in life, she had tempered an ordinary intuition into a kind of clairvoyance, and by the time her child was born she could play a hunch for a sure thing.

And so, instead of grief, Susan found the emotional preparedness that comes with foreknowledge. She had realized years earlier that her husband's primary sense of responsibility was to alcohol and had built up around herself the invisible walls that allowed her to preserve her family and save herself. Dan never saw much past the rim of his glass anyway and so had scarcely noticed the barrier she placed between them.

*

The windows were closed against the afternoon's rain, and as Susan chewed on the end of her pen, the smell of the cleanser she'd been mopping with filled her sinuses. It made her feel efficient and vaguely cheerful. She picked up the notepad, jotted down the number of their lawyer and some of the questions she had for him, then looked up and saw that Jonah, who'd been in the backyard, was now inside and tracking mud across the kitchen. He was walking a stuffed dog, pulling it with a length of twine and erasing his small muddy footprints with a long, brown streak.

She looked up. Jonah was standing in front of her.

"Honey," she said, "listen to me. Your father is dead."

Jonah looked up at her. The beauty of his wide, clear eyes was more than she could bear and she pulled him to her. Undeterred by the news of his father's death and suffocating calmly between his mother's breasts, Jonah continued the wait he'd begun the day his father hadn't shown for his party.

*

Susan stayed up later than usual that night wondering what she was supposed to be feeling. She drank the remainder of Dan's bourbon, musing that it was almost certainly the last bottle the house would ever see, and let her thoughts wander, not missing Dan so much as wondering why the men in her life kept dying. Her dad's plane had gone down en route to Da Nang. Her first fiancé had drowned in a boating accident the summer of their junior year. And now Dan.

When she reached the bottom of the bottle she laughed out loud at her tendency, regardless of the situation, to think about her dad. His memory was so strong sometimes it was as if he were standing right next to her.

*

Before she passed out, Susan fell to staring at her right hand. She'd lost her index and middle fingers to a table saw in college and still couldn't figure out where they'd gone.

*

Jonah did not want to go to his father's funeral. Not because he didn't believe that his father was really dead; going to the funeral of someone who was going to show up at any minute made as much sense as anything else adults made him do. He didn't want to go because of the suit his mother was making him wear. For one, it was navy blue. The worst color on earth. For two, the collar was too tight and it made him feel like he was in a choke hold. For three, the pants were loose, but the waist gripped him too high on his hairless body and it made him feel funny. And for four, it was navy blue. The worst color on earth. Jonah glowered back at the idiot boy in the mirror. Transported by disgust, he pulled his shoulders in, stretching the fabric across his back, feeling the suit bite at his armpits, testing the seams by degree until, finally, one of them gave. Jonah straightened up and, caught irrevocably between his rage and the fact that he would get it if he wrecked his clothes, vented his spite by eking three drops of urine out of his penis and into the suit. Not enough to show, but enough to lodge the complaint with God.

*

Susan was far more comfortable in her suit. She did not, however, relish the thought of having to appear bereaved for the sake of those who would come to pay their respects. The whole thing was a nuisance really, but, she supposed, a necessary one. Susan sipped her coffee and stretched out diagonally on her huge bed, lying still while the morning sunshine warmed her clothes. It wouldn't be so bad. And it would be over soon enough. Then they could come back home and she and Jonah would have the house and the afternoon to themselves. As she sifted through what she knew would happen that day, the thought of her and her son, unhurried as they made their way through another summer's day, made her feel happy and relaxed. She smiled, linked her hands behind her head, and recrossed her feet. Poor little Jonah. She closed her eyes and thought about her son, about that smart little suit she'd picked for him, about his smooth, soft forehead wrinkling as he concentrated on his shoelaces. He was growing up so quickly. Her mind drifted back to nighttime feedings, alone in Jonah's moonlit nursery, while her baby suckled and the rest of the world slept.

*

"Do you know where we're going, honey?"

"Uh-huh." Jonah was looking out the car window but wasn't seeing much more than the tops of the trees. Susan was concentrating on the road.

"Can you tell me what it's called?"

"A foon-earl."

"A funeral, that's right. Can you remember why we're doing it?"

"To help us not be sad and . . ."

". . . and to mark a rite of passage with a ritual."

Jonah slumped further down in the seat so that the shoulder strap caught him at the neck. He was wondering about the tinted part at the top of the windshield.

"And do you know why we do that, Jonah?"

"To not be sad?"

"To help others not be sad. We do it to help others. So when people talk to you today, remember that we're doing all this for them." Susan caught her son's eyes for a moment, but then had to look back at the road. Jonah looked at his legs.

"'Kay. Mom?"

"Yes?"

"Who's gonna be there?"

"People like us. People who are sad that Daddy's dead."

"Is Dad gonna be there?"

Susan thought about it.

"Yeah. Dad'll be there too."

Jonah straightened up and began to pay attention to where they were going.

*

There were no walls apparent in the funeral parlor, just curtains and doors, and although there was no chink through which sunlight could slip, there were plants everywhere. Jonah reached up to grab one of the huge plastic ferns on a display shelf in the entryway and just as he touched the tip of one long, green leaf, he lost his balance and brought the plant, pot and all, down onto his head.

When she heard the crash, Susan turned from the funeral director and ran to her son.

"Jonah! What are you doing?"

Jonah didn't give an answer, knowing full well that his mother didn't want one.

"Jonah, you're bleeding! Mr. Stevenson, get me some paper towels, some antiseptic, and some Band-Aids!"

His mother barking orders helped Jonah gather some of his attention, and he reached up to touch the spot where the falling vase had split the skin of his forehead. He furrowed his brow, feeling the dull sting at either end of the cut and watching the blood as it dripped off his check in fat droplets. He could also see Mr. Stevenson, scuttling to and fro at his mother's behest. His mother was still talking and Jonah began to listen.

". . . don't know why you insist on communicating your feelings indirectly. Wouldn't it be easier to just tell me you're upset because of the funeral? Why can't you . . ."

"Mom, where's Dad?"

"Oh, Jonah, honestly, I thought we'd . . ."

Susan was dabbing forcefully at his forehead with paper towels and hydrogen peroxide and Jonah stopped paying attention. Mr. Stevenson hovered nervously over his mother's shoulder, shifting his weight from one foot to the other and sending nervous glances from side to side. One of the glances caught the scattered flowers and broken glass and Jonah saw the man swoop over to the mess, gather it between his hands, and take it in several quick trips over to a trash can hidden in a wall recess behind a burgundy curtain. Trying to hold his head steady against the repeated pressure of his mother's attentions, Jonah wondered at the dexterity adults seemed to possess that allowed them to pick up broken glass without cutting themselves.

The first of the mourners arrived and with a word to Susan, Mr. Stevenson hurried off to greet them.

"Mrs. Hart, if you would be so kind as to take your place . . ."

"Okay, Jonah, now I know you're upset, but I want you to listen to me, okay? Honey? Listen. Daddy's friends are starting to arrive, so we have to go and sit down. Now, if something's upsetting you, I want you to feel free to talk to me about it later on, okay? If you don't want to, that's okay too, but if you want to, you can. Okay? You're very important to me, Jonah."

Susan leaned forward to kiss the Band-Aid she'd placed over Jonah's cut, hoping to underscore her point with a little affection, but as she put her lips to the plastic and found her nose filled with the smell of his scalp, she lost control, pulled him to her, and buried as much of her face as she could in his thin hair. She could feel his ribs and shoulder blades through his suit as she hugged him. She pulled herself away and sighed sharply, using her wrists to wipe away the tears that had formed.

*

Though Dan Hart looked natural and relaxed at his funeral, he did not look a thing like himself. This was due mostly to the fact that on his way into the next world, he had left half of his face on the windshield. Reassured by an enthusiastic young embalmer who claimed he could work from photographs, and believing that a closed-casket funeral was the same as no funeral at all, Susan had consented to the reconstruction knowing that even the most sincere efforts could not capture Dan's primary features: the smile on his face, the veins on his cheeks, and the drink in his hand.

Behind Susan and Jonah, friends and associates arrived and slid into place, filling the chapel with muffled conversation, the creaking of wooden pews, an occasional cough, and, less occasionally, the sound of laughter. The room was lit by carefully situated stage lights, which shone down in blue, purple, and gold, and were intended to simulate the feel of stained glass. Two single shafts of white light coming down out of the darkness drew the attention of the mourners to the casket, surrounded by flowers, the few sent by friends bolstered by selections from the funeral home's permanent collection. Usually the temperature in the room sat at a comfortable sixty-seven degrees, but due to a glitch in the thermostat, it was now careening back and forth between fifty-five and eighty. People were sticking to their clothes one minute, noticing a cold sweat the next.

The house lights dimmed and Mr. Stevenson appeared at the pulpit. When the silence was complete, he began.

*

". . . knowing we all come here today with a burden to share. The love we had for . . ." He paused. "Dan . . . has become our grief . . ."

". . . for in our dreams of what might have been, feelings of grief can turn into feelings of guilt, both for things done and things left undone. But, you know something? That's okay. Each and every one of us can turn to the other and say, 'Hey, it's okay . . .'"

*

The delight began at the very center of Jonah's soul and welled up within him as he sat bolt upright, transfixed by the sight in front of him. Even his expectation hadn't prepared him for this, and it was pushing the hair along the back of his neck up into little vibrating points. There, seated at the end of his own casket, looking fresh out of the shower with his thin hair combed straight back, a grin on his face and a drink in his hand, was his father. He caught Jonah's eye, and in the moment that he held it, winked. Jonah, smiling at the congregation like it was his birthday and they'd just surprised him with a party, left his seat and went to go sit next to his dad.

*

Inside the casket, nestled momentarily with his father, Jonah supplied the particulars of the birthday party he'd missed.

". . . and Ben was there and and we waited and waited, but you still weren't there, so Mom gave us cake."

Snuggling against the wool of his father's suit, Jonah continued, oblivious to the riot that approached. "Dad, why did you have to go?"

"Don't worry about it, kid. I'll be around. The apple doesn't fall too far from the tree, you know."

Jonah had no idea what his father was talking about, contenting himself with the sound of his father's voice. He was trying to formulate a response when many hands grabbed him and he was borne away.

*

"Jonah! There you are! Where on earth have you been?"

Jonah didn't have an answer for his mom. It just felt good to sit in the still darkness. But the calm was ruined when his mom pulled the burgundy curtain back. He looked up at her and answered.

"I dunno."

"Well, why are you in the trash can?"

"I dunno."

"Don't you want to get out?"

"I guess so."

Jonah stepped out and his mother gasped. He had been kneeling in the shards from the broken pot and had dozens of cuts up and down his pale legs.

"Jonah, not again."

Jonah was surprised too. He hadn't noticed.

*

YOUNG SALMONHOOD

FOR AS LONG AS ANYONE COULD REMEMBER, people had been coming to the waterfall. That's why there was trash everywhere. Rings of it had been left by high water, circling the basin like seats in an amphitheater. Beyond, the woods were pristine pine trees and deep beds of needles.

Jonah and his friends would have called this time of the year fall because they were back in school, but the hot September Saturday was summer as deep as summer gets. Laughing, shouting, and following the main path that led from the road to the falls, they passed through the woods, unaware of the silence that parted at their coming and closed in behind them as they left. When the sound of the falls could just be heard over the silence of the trees, the path forked and the three boys turned right. They walked in single file along the tip of the ravine to the small, bald ridge that would allow them to leap out past the jagged rocks and into the only part of the stream where the water was deep enough.

The four girls went left, carrying the stuff, chatting amongst themselves.

"I swear to God, one of these days, one of those guys is gonna get killed."

"I know."

"I swear."

"I mean, are they retards, or what?"

*

"Oh my God, this is *so* good." Sandra chewed in ecstasy.

"See what I mean?" Kim said.

"Oh my God, it's so grape."

"What are you guys talking about?" Ross, freshly emerged from the water, was dripping it in trickles onto the sun-warmed rock. Sandra's undulations at how good it was drew the boys to her. At fourteen she was completely developed and the fullness of the movement beneath her bikini had a couple of them seated with their legs crossed.

"Mmmm! Mmmm-mmmm! Kim, you tell them."

"Well," Kim said, reaching into one of the bags and rummaging for demonstration materials, "if you put the grape candy in your mouth and don't bite it . . ."

Ross cracked into his immediately and Kim had to give him another one.

". . . when you eat the grape bubblegum at the same time, it tastes *really* grape."

They all followed suit. Sandra was right—it was the grapest thing they'd ever tasted.

*

Kim picked up their trash while the rest of them got ready to leave. The sun had moved behind the trees and the evening air held the first hints of autumn briskness that make it feel cold even though it really isn't. Summer was sliding off their part of the planet, and winter was approaching, gradually and without stealth.

*

Ross shivered, arms crossed around his chest, legs close together. Lost in thought, he hadn't realized that the others were leaving. Jonah approached him.

"Hey Ross, you okay? Ross?"

"Huh?"

"You okay?"

"Oh, yeah, I'm fine. I'm just really cold."

"Want to wear my jacket?"

It was obvious from his expression that he wanted to.

"Naw, that's okay. What would you wear?"

"Nothing. I mean, I'm not cold. It's warm out."

"Are you sure? It's your favorite coat and everything."

Jonah's mom had bought it for his fifteenth birthday, two weeks ago. She'd contacted Ross and arranged to have him take her to all the places where kids shopped these days. They'd settled on an oversized mechanics coat, very expensive and very cool. Jonah liked it, he guessed. He'd gone out the day after his birthday feeling slightly silly in such an obviously fashionable piece of clothing, but when everyone he ran into commented on what a great jacket it was, he'd figured he must look okay.

"I'm sure. Here."

Ross took it reluctantly and then proudly pulled it on. Though a bit too tight around Ross's broader shoulders, it actually looked much better on him. He'd picked it out.

"Thanks a lot, Jonah. God, this is a great jacket."

"You want it?"

"Huh?"

"You can have it if you want it. You want it?"

"Well, yeah, but . . ."

"Hey, who's that?"

"Who's what?"

"Up there."

"I don't see anybody."

But Jonah did.

*

A woman stood alone on the cliff above them, watching the others as they made their way along the path. Her suit was aqua and her long, pale arms hung limply from her shoulders. As she followed their movements, Jonah could see that, beneath a tilting bouffant, most of the back of her head was gone. She turned slowly to look at the two boys who remained by the falls, and Jonah saw the blackened hole of an entrance wound right between her eyes. Her chest was still pointed toward the group; she had turned only her head to catch Jonah's gaze. She held it for a moment, then smiled. And winked. Jonah pissed himself, right then and there, and when he realized what he was doing, he leapt back into the water. Ross gaped at him, incredulous.

"Jonah, we just got out."

"So?"

"So why did you jump back in?"

"I wanted to swim."

"You're weird Jonah. Really weird."

Jonah, in water up to his waist, didn't say anything.

*

"Ten o'clock, Jonah."

Jonah ignored his mother, concentrating instead on the commercial for Total cereal, one bowl of which was apparently as nutritious as ten bowls of another leading brand.

"*Jonah, ten o'clock.*" His mother was singing her words now, which meant she was through fucking around.

"Huh?" If he acted now, Time/Life would include a telephone, free.

"Jonah. Bedtime."

Jonah turned and looked at his mother.

*

Every evening after dinner Susan and her son would study together, Jonah because he had to and Susan because she loved it. Aggressively autodidactic, she'd failed out of virtually every school she'd ever attended, not through laziness or inability, but because she'd inevitably invent tougher and more interesting assignments for herself and turn those in instead. The books that lined the long walls of the living room represented years of research and cross-referencing and, to her knowledge, constituted the best working library of anyone she knew.

Susan was single-minded in her intensity, though scattered in her tastes. There were the technical manuals and journals that Susan found useful in her job as a film editor. There was also a huge section of interrelated texts on psycholinguistics, neuro-linguistic programming, self-hypnosis and other methods of mind control. This fed naturally into psychology, which, though it started with Freud and Jung, was dominated by behaviorists. In anthropology, things were mostly Stone Age: Yanomamo, Mbuti, !Kung—Susan once had it in her mind to learn how it had been before it all got fucked up, but soon tossed the notion, concluding that things have never been *not* fucked up. History, philosophy, and sociology were all mixed up in a messy section of which Susan could never quite bring herself to be proud. By far, the biggest and most commanding sections of the library were reserved for erotica and books on guns. There were no novels.

While her son studied, Susan would pore over her latest set of books, referencing them against other titles when something rang a bell and outlining everything on the laptop whose screen-saver idled hypnotically on the ottoman just to her right. When Jonah was done with his studies, she would monitor what TV shows he watched with one eye while continuing to study with the other.

When Jonah looked at his mother in that room, he saw mostly her high-backed wicker plantation chair. An heirloom from a Confederate ancestor, it was Susan's prized possession, the only thing her father had refused to give her while he was still alive. In Jonah's mind's eye, that was where she always sat—sipping coffee and telling him what to do.

There was no point in arguing. He'd done that before, many times, and the result was always the same. Her point of view carried the weight of authority and tilted the discussion, so that no matter what he said, he was always downhill from his mother.

With a sigh, he started up the steps.

"No kiss?" Susan was smiling, resplendent.

Jonah returned and gave her the kiss.

"'Night, Mom."

"'Night, love."

*

As he made his way up the steps he could hear his mother in the kitchen, putting away the dishes they had left out to dry. When she was through with that, she would make their lunches. At the top of the steps Jonah stopped and listened to his mother's busy clatter.

*

Dishes done, lunches made, kitchen clean, Susan surveyed her handiwork. Satisfied, she flicked the light switch as she left the room, returning to her chair. After she saved her work to a disk, she reshelved the books taken down during that evening's study, lingering in each section, letting her thoughts wander. It was her final ritual of the evening. Positioned in front of her erotica collection, Susan went from spine to spine without reading, noticing instead the colors and stopping occasionally to feel the texture. She made her selection as if sleeping, cradling the book absently. Forsaking the autodidactic for the autoerotic, Susan went upstairs to bed.

*

For as long as Jonah could remember having dreams at all, the first one of the night had always been what he called "the warm one." He would pass from drowsiness into actual sleep on what felt like a body of warm water that would cover him like his blankets and whose currents would carry him to the place where he would do the rest of his dreaming. It was a pleasant feeling, one that would swell up around him and take his body away by degrees. Sleep would leave him and he would pass into a world that was entirely his own. He liked it, and at an early age had learned to cultivate it.

By age seven, Jonah would purposefully submerge in his bed at night, relaxing his body limb by limb and bringing the water up around him. From there he could do as he pleased, usually drifting a while before moving along toward the dream place, sifting through the faces and occurrences of the day, then moving deeper to where things were unpredictable and puzzling. There was nothing unusual about the dreams besides their stunning clarity and how refreshed they would leave him. So he kept them as his secret.

*

Sleep came as it always did, like the sun out from behind a cloud, and Jonah felt good, deeply relaxed and ready. He was floating, drifting idly, calmly eager for a night of dreams when, without knowing how, Jonah unhooked from the dream and floated out of it. Nothing like this had ever happened before. He was staring at the ceiling, wondering what to do, and when he turned around, he looked down and saw himself, sleeping.

*

He floated there for some time. This was no dream, but he was asleep; the proof was below. Every time he began to panic, the feeling would dissipate as he watched himself draw long, slow breaths. Eventually, he found himself staring out the window, down at the streetlit cars and houses. Half of everything was in shadow, half was bright and flat. The only way he could imagine describing it was that he could see grass growing and metal rusting; or, rather, he could see things changing into what they would become. It was deeply beautiful.

Floating still, Jonah moved along the second floor hallway and down the steps, following the path he used when he walked even as he realized that he was absolutely unbound. The wood of the house grew brittle beneath paint that was turning to dust, root-bound houseplants strained against clay pots, electricity flowed within coated wire in a rush of positive and negative ions. It was all visible and, without the limitations of his physical body, Jonah found it comprehensible. His mother's chair was still warm with her presence, but the room, bent by the angling bars of shadow and moonlight, was cold. Jonah could see the moon, framed by the tall oaks that lined the yard, as it traveled across the sky, reflecting the light of the sun, which he could feel beneath the spinning earth.

*

Jonah hurried through the doors of his first period class.

"Late again, Mr. Hart?"

"Sorry, Mr. Erlichmann. I mean, yes. I am. Late. Sorry."

"Everyone, I want you to look at Jonah. He has exhibited an amazing consistency. Every day since the year began, he has been late. Every single day. It fascinates me. Jonah, are you late for your other classes?"

"No sir."

"And you attend homeroom?"

"Yes sir."

"Then, do tell us, why are you late for this, the first class of your day?"

"I don't know."

"You don't know?"

At this point it was customary for Jonah to say nothing while the class waited in gleeful anticipation of whatever put-down Erlichmann was going to conjure up for that day. It was invariably more interesting than *American History for Young Americans* by

Silverman, Henderson, Isaacs, and Tole, and, in the same way that a man who constantly punishes his dog makes you wonder about him and not the animal, the daily diversion left most of the kids grateful to Jonah and rather skeptical concerning the validity of anything their teacher might say for the rest of the period.

"Well, if *you* don't know, I don't know who would!"

The class rustled with amusement and Jonah smiled sheepishly in response to the admiring glances of his classmates. Erlichmann shuffled papers with his back to the class to let his point sink in. The class looked at the clock or out the window until Erlichmann turned back and began his lecture.

"Okay, follow along with me. You're in Jamestown and it's 1609 . . ."

*

Jonah was late every day not because of delinquency or lack of respect on his part, but because a dead janitor, obscenely fat and naked from the waist down, was harassing him in the hallway on his way to class. Soon after he had seen the ghost at the waterfall, the janitor had shown up, milling about with the students on their way to class. Jonah, still new to the ghost thing, stood stunned as he realized that nobody else cared because no one could see him. The guy was dead.

It had been an otherwise normal moment. Kids leaned against lockers, chatting. Opposing lanes of students meandered toward class. The morning sun shone through the windows at the far end of the hall, making everyone squint. Except Jonah. His eyes were open as far as they could go. So was his mouth. In fact, so were the valves of his heart—beating in overdrive just this side of cardiac arrest. He couldn't move even though a couple of kids had bumped into him and he knew in the very back of his mind that they must be staring. And when the ghost realized that one of these kids could actually see him, Jonah beheld a rage released from the constraints of being alive and, in the same helpless way he had been rooted to the floor, Jonah fled, regardless of who or what he might bump into. He ended up outside, on the shady end of the building, hidden between the dumpster and the service shed, and when he calmed down enough to feel the bruises rising on his shins and shoulders, he wept in abject hopelessness about never being able to go anywhere, ever again.

*

Over time, Jonah learned that although the janitor would undergo knee-weakening facial contortions in the presence of someone who could see him, this was all he was capable of. Soon Jonah figured out that if he hid in the bathroom near his homeroom until the halls cleared, he could skirt away from the ghost and avoid the scrutiny of his schoolmates. It made him late for his first period class, but it worked. That is, it had worked until today. Today the ghost had started moving toward him. Only two steps, but it had Jonah worried. Until now, the janitor had seemed caught up in the flow of traffic and Jonah found that he could pass him at the spot where the flow washed him up. He had grown so used to the idea that the ghost was at the mercy of the tide that he was even beginning to mock the guy who had once frightened him so absolutely. But today, the dead guy had moved, first one and then the other of his skinny gray legs, and his expression, which Jonah found terrifying again, had expanded to include a small measure of hope.

*

As Erlichmann lectured, Jonah thought about the crawl space at Ross's house that ran behind his sister's room. The week before, they were following the cat so they could get the beer cans off its legs before Ross's mom came home, and they had found themselves listening through the wall to Ross's sister, Gabrielle, and her friend Cindy talk about menstruation. They went back the next day and the two girls, who had been joined by a third, were talking about birth control. Jonah and Ross couldn't believe it. Sweating in the dark, they eavesdropped with the faraway look of people listening to radio in the days before television. Ross was getting nervous, but Jonah knew that a little peer pressure could have them right back at it. He spun on his seat to leer at Ross, who was sitting behind him, but found himself looking instead at the girl who was sitting one row back. She was looking straight at him. Smiling.

His first reaction was to spin around and play nonchalant. His second reaction was to turn and double-check to make sure she wasn't dead, but his third reaction was to abort the second reaction, because if she were alive, he'd come off like a total geek if he turned around again without a plan. So he checked her out in his mind, which he would have done anyway since her image was blinding him like the flash from a camera. Not only was she alive—she was cute. She was small and athletic looking, with red hair pulled back in a ponytail and an abbreviated, upturned nose that said tomboy all over it. And she was smiling at him. He tried to make out what was going on underneath her sweater, but the image was unclear in that department. Then, completely unable to concentrate, he turned his attention back to Erlichmann.

*

When the second-hand passed the twelve for the fiftieth time, the bell rang and Jonah dove into action. He had no idea what to do, so he just stood there, making a triangle out of himself, Ross, and the girl. She gathered her things, Ross scratched himself, and Jonah searched the situation for the slightest clue as to what he was supposed to do. The girl smiled contentedly to herself in a way that led Jonah to believe that she knew he was watching and was pretending not to notice. Ross was grimacing, trying to get a better angle on the itch between his shoulder blades. Jonah admired the girl's hands and how deftly she stacked her books in descending order according to size. Having made everything just so, she hefted the books to her chest, raised her head, and, still smiling, looked Jonah squarely in the eye.

"See you later."

She was halfway out of the classroom before it dawned on Jonah that he might want to respond in some way.

"Yeah! See you!"

He'd yelled it and three of his friends between him and the door thought he was talking to them and waved. The girl kept smiling, then opened the door by backing into it, turned, and was gone. The door flapped in her wake.

"Hi Jonah," Ross said.

Jonah punched him on the tender part of his arm, just below the shoulder muscle.

"Ow! What'ya do that for?"

"Who is she?" Jonah asked, finally feeling like himself again.

"Who's who?" Ross was rubbing his arm with the same confused expression he'd had while searching for the itch.

"The girl who sits right here."

"Her name's Sara. She's from Iowa. Weren't you here on the day we went around and introduced ourselves?"

Jonah ignored the question. He was trying to remember everything he knew about Iowa. All he could come up with was corn.

"Why do you want to know, anyway?"

"No reason."

"You like her!" Ross said it with the enthusiasm usually reserved for "*Aha!*"

"No way!"

"Yes way! Jonah's in love!" He sang it loud enough for everyone to hear.

"Dude. No way."

Ross looked at his friend in mock disapproval. "We're going to have to give you a make-over . . ."

"Hey, are we going to go listen to your sister this afternoon?"

"Jonah, I already told you . . ."

They walked toward the door together. Erlichmann shuffled papers on his desk, getting ready for next period. Ross blathered on.

"I mean, we could do it one more time, but you've got to promise . . ."

Everyone else was gone. The sun shone indirectly through the screened windows and the room was still and quiet. Until Jonah screamed.

"Jonah, have you gone mad?" asked Erlichmann.

"Yeah, Jonah, are you okay?" Ross was holding the door open, oblivious to the dead man standing behind him.

"I'm fine. My, um, mother's birthday is today. I totally forgot. That's all."

It was a lie. But it was also a masterpiece of self-control and ingenuity, made all the more impressive by the fact that every muscle in his body was involved in clenching the jaw through which he'd squeezed the words. Jonah stood with his head down, keeping the janitor's bare feet just inside the rim of his peripheral vision, afraid that if he saw more he'd start screaming again. Erlichmann returned to his papers and his memories. Ross was looking at Jonah with genuine concern.

"But I'll get her something after school. Okay, let's go."

Ross started off, hesitantly. Jonah gestured with his palms as if to say, "After you." Then, head still down, he slipped around him as they passed the janitor and walked down the hall.

"You're weird, Jonah."

Jonah was busy not looking back and so, said nothing.

*

Ross played quarterback. Ross always played quarterback. Jonah, by default, was the rest of the team. Ross exhaled into his cupped hands, warming them against the chill of the moist fall day, and narrated as the two-man team lined up against their imaginary opponents.

"Williams tries to quiet the crowd, but they won't shut up! They're freaking out because these Washington Redskins are about to clinch the biggest Super Bowl victory ever in the history of mankind!" Ross looked back and forth over the front line. "10-41! 10-41! Blue! Blue! Hike!" The words echoed against the tall brick walls of the high school and across the deserted playing field. Jonah snapped the ball and followed a slant pattern to the left corner of the end zone where his diving catch would have the most dramatic impact.

"Monk's open in the corner! Monk in the corner!" Ross threw the ball, but it went wide, and Jonah, who was standing tiptoe just in bounds, couldn't reach it. Ignoring the dead cheerleaders limping through a series of antique cheers on the running track that surrounded the field, Jonah ran for the ball. They reset and Ross constructed the scenario again.

"Redskins! Super Bowl! Fourth and goal! Go!"

This time the ball hit him right on the palms. He tucked it into his chest as the grass rose to meet him, and when he got up, the crowd was going wild. Ross came running up and the two of them whooped and did victory dances until they had to lie down.

"Man, I'm tired."

"Me too."

"It's getting dark."

"Yeah."

They'd been having nowhere conversations like that all day. Jonah knew Ross had something to tell him because normally Ross never shut up. Unless there was something on his mind, in which case he worried his concerns in silence.

"Think fast!"

Ross lofted the ball up into a tall arc so that it would land with plenty of force on Jonah, who lay in the damp grass two feet away. Jonah rolled out from under him and the two of them scrambled for the ball. Soon they were tossing it back and forth again. Whereupon Ross got around to the point.

"So you like Sara Benson." Ross threw the ball as he said it.

"Who told you that?" Jonah caught it and threw it back.

"Sandra."

"Oh," Jonah said, catching the ball against his chest.

Ross caught Jonah's next toss, then paused to speak before he unloaded.

"Sandra also said that Sara really likes you."

"She does?"

Jonah dropped his hands in amazement and the incoming football bonked him right on the forehead.

*

Jonah never learned why, but for some reason hardware stores attracted more ghosts than other places, even graveyards and old abandoned houses, which it turned out weren't any more popular than anywhere else. Movie theaters drew more than their share. Bad neighborhoods had a lot. But it was hardware stores that drew them in droves. Much of what he came to know of ghosts and dreams he learned only in retrospect, but the correlation between ghosts and hardware stores was something he picked up on right away.

Every weekend for the last year and a half, his mother, as a part of her ongoing lifestyle project, had dragged Jonah to the hardware store, where the two of them would buy the various supplies they'd need for the do-it-yourself project Susan had researched in preparation for that weekend. Simple stuff mostly, space-saving utility shelves, easy-to-install ventilation systems, three-step furniture refinishing, et cetera, all intended to provide Jonah with a sense of accomplishment and an idea of what he could do if he just set his mind to it. What he got, though, was the kind of training they give police horses to keep them from being startled. A hardware store on a Saturday is bad enough. With twice as many people, half of them dead, it's another thing entirely. Jonah was learning to keep his cool, even in the valley of the shadow of death, and in that sense, it was a valuable experience. But, like most valuable experiences, Jonah would have avoided it if he could.

Even more disconcerting than the ghosts were the fingers, knuckles, hands, and occasional forearms that would inch their way across the store en route to the room where they sold the shop tools used by contractors. Every hardware store had them, thousands of them, piled on and around all the table saws and planers, radial arm saws and joiners—the serious tools, powerful, precise, and absolutely unable to differentiate between lumber and flesh. Every Saturday, he would see two or three more inch their way across the store to their resting place.

*

The October sky was slate gray, the leaves had turned, and occasional drops of rain fell at forty-five-degree angles, each driven by the wind to its own little ground zero. Jonah got out of his mother's Isuzu Trooper, and as he started to make his way across the parking lot, a drop hit him at the corner of his eye.

"You've got the list, right Jonah?"

"Yes, Mom."

"Good. Now make sure the man rips the plywood exactly . . ."

They'd been over it all before, so Jonah kept an eye out for corpses. On a day like today it was easy, the live folk were the ones hurrying to get out of the rain, and the dead were the ones milling about the lot like teenagers with nothing to do. Mostly, they hung out in small groups, looking inside empty cars. A few walked slowly toward the store. There were about forty of them altogether, a few of whom were really young.

". . . are we agreed?" his mother finished.

"Sure."

"Okay, now hurry. I want to have time to get to the shooting range—you're sure you don't want to come?" Susan asked this question every Saturday.

"No thanks."

"I wish you'd reconsider, Jonah. You know, when my daddy taught me how to shoot . . ."

Jonah waited patiently as his mother spoke.

*

None of the employees wanted to come outside, so the pumpkins and Indian corn on display along the front of the store lay in complete disarray. A couple of the smaller pumpkins rolled loose—perfect obstacles to the people carrying purchases to their cars in the pick-up lane.

The onset of all the Halloween and autumnal-equinox merchandise presented Jonah with a lot of red herrings. For instance, over in the corner, at the edge of the display, a figure of a man with white work gloves and a jack-o'-lantern head sat in a chair. Was this a seasonal amusement for the weekend shoppers, or a fiend from hell come to scare the shit out of him? Jonah was halfway across the pick-up lane when old Jack recrossed his legs and slumped down a little lower in his chair, confirming the latter. Jonah had been bracing himself for his first shock ever since he'd gotten out of the car. Even so, the fear rose from his stomach like steam, and he had to stand very still in an effort to keep it from rising into his mouth where it would become a scream. It was then that he noticed that the fiend wasn't wearing white work gloves after all. The things at the ends of his arms were regular hands, just really swollen and pale.

The man trying to get by in his van was on his third honk before Jonah noticed him, at which point Susan, who had gone ahead, came back out of the store to rescue him. She led him gently onto the curb and knelt down in front of him.

"Honey? You okay?"

"Stomachache."

Susan sighed and reached up to stroke her son's hair where it was shaved close on the side.

"Honey, I'm going to have to insist that we go see a doctor about these stomachaches of yours. Okay?"

"Sure. Yeah. Good idea."

*

The situation was no better inside the hardware store, but it was warmer at least. Jonah looked around, preparing himself for the next shock. The high ceilings and open spaces of the store reminded Jonah of his school cafeteria, only it had muzak piped in and, of course, it smelled like hardware instead of food. People rushed about in varying states of determination and confusion—unless they were dead, in which case they just stood around, looking at stuff. Each cashier had two or three dead folk with him behind the register. Some of the dead waited in the long lines with the live folk. Others sat in shopping carts waiting for someone to give them a ride. They were everywhere. Just hanging around.

"Jonah?"

The boy started at the sound of his mother's voice. He looked up and saw a balding man who looked like he must have died in a discotheque circa 1975 standing next to her, staring at her hands.

"Jonah, I need you to get the plywood cut to our specifications. Also, could you pick out a new trash can while they're cutting it?"

"Sure thing, Mom."

Susan walked off, leaving Jonah with Disco Man. Jonah was afraid to look at his face, so he kept tabs by looking at the man's feet, clad in orange and brown shoes with two-inch-high stacked heels.

*

Ghosts were confusing because there didn't seem to be any rules governing their behavior. As soon as Jonah thought he had it all figured out and knew what to expect some ghost would come along and do precisely the opposite. For instance, in his experience, ghosts had never been able to make noise or move much, and yet, here was Disco Man, whistling a song Jonah didn't recognize and dancing in an obscene, though quite fluid fashion. And the clothes they wore didn't make any sense. Some, like the old folk in hospital smocks, were obviously wearing what they'd died in, but others wore suits and dresses only appropriate for burials. And some smelled really terrible. It just didn't make any sense.

*

Disco Man whistled up to the chorus, then began singing in a strange, soulless falsetto.

"Whether you're a mother or whether you're a lover, it's stayin' alive, stayin' alive . . ."

Jonah shot him a look, but he was already dancing off down the aisle. Digging in his pocket for his list, Jonah followed after the ghost toward the back exit and the lumberyard.

*

The guys in the lumberyard had grown quite fond of Jonah. Luther and Carl, whom Jonah called Mr. Burnett and Mr. Simms, had taken pity on this skinny kid who was openly in awe of what they did and as fascinated by the yard as he was afraid to ask for help of any kind. When Mr. Burnett gave Jonah his table saw safety speech and showed him the three shorn knuckles on his right hand, it was only the second time Mr. Simms had seen him do that in the five years he'd been working there.

"'Morning, Mr. Simms."

"Jonah! How you doing this morning?"

"Fine, thanks. Hey, Mr. Burnett."

"Hey there, Jonah. Nice haircut."

"Thanks."

"Barber do that on purpose?"

The two men exploded with laughter. Jonah hid his grin by showing it to his feet.

While he waited, he watched the ghosts play in the sawdust. They gathered behind the big table saw where the sawdust was allowed to collect, crawling on all fours like cattle. Something about the dust was intoxicating to them. They'd stare at it, rub it into their skin and hair, try to press it back into wood, and watch it slip between their fingers as they separated their cupped hands.

*

The yard was huge, stack after stack of lumber piled beneath gently ascending awnings. Along the side that shared a wall and a loading dock with the main building, saws and customers vied for Luther and Carl's attention. The center of the yard was exposed to the elements like a courtyard, pine and plywood stacked high in long racks, leaving just enough room to maneuver the forklifts. Luther and Carl had their blue Ballard Lumber windbreakers pulled in snug.

"What you need today, Jonah?"

Jonah handed Carl his list and the man mumbled as he read it.

"Okay. It's going to be a little while, though. If you've got some other stuff to get, you should go on."

*

Alone in the long wide aisle, Jonah studied the trash cans. They seemed to come in three basic colors of plastic: light blue, off pink, and pale tan. These colors, the plastic smell of the new cans, and the glare from the fluorescent light conspired to give Jonah a headache. All he wanted was your basic garbage can, but there didn't seem to be any such thing. He stepped back to take it all in, put his heel on something unseen, lost his balance, and fell flat, buried amongst the rows of trash cans he'd waded into. When he got his wits back about him, he looked to see what he had tripped on and saw that it was a finger. And that it was pointing at him.

He felt a tickling at his spine, jerked around, and saw a second finger inchworming toward him. Squealing in disgust, he wrapped his arms around his shoulders and began shuffling backwards at the same pace as the finger's inchings forward until, with a frantic glance over his shoulder, he saw a third finger coming up behind him, cutting off his avenue of escape. He had no idea what to do, so he turned the decision over to his body, which jumped into one of the trash cans, the big round kind that sit out in the alley, and gripped the rim as hard as it could.

Thirty or forty seconds passed. Jonah wished frantically for a gun, then felt a wave of self-loathing at such a stupid thought. Like I'm gonna kill dead fingers.

The fingers just lay there, enjoying their tactical advantage.

"Jonah! Hey Jonah!"

It was Sara Benson, smiling and waving and coming straight toward Jonah and his three new friends. This time her ponytail was complemented by corduroys and a rain parka, both white. Her hair, wet from the rain, gave her the glowing good looks of someone who had just showered. Of course, Jonah could not appreciate this, in the same way you can't appreciate a gourmet meal if the person next to you is making sucking noises with his eggs. The fingers held their position, waiting to see what would happen, and Jonah struggled with the task of watching four things at once.

Sara strode up, placed herself in front of the trembling Jonah, and put her hands right on the rim of the can in which he was standing. Holding on, she leaned back slightly, blushing, smiling, and looking him right in the eyes.

"Hey, Jonah. How's it going?"

"Hey, Sara. Fine. Great. Real great."

"Do you have something in your eye?"

"No."

"Oh. Nevermind."

One of the fingers had disappeared and Jonah was trying to locate it without moving his head.

"Jonah?"

"Yes?"

"How come you're standing in the trash can?"

"Well, you've got to test them out to see if they're any good."

He began stomping and giving the inside of the can a critical eye. Sara's expression changed to show that although she had no idea what on earth Jonah was doing, she was still just as happy to be standing next to him as she had been before he'd started stomping.

"So how come you're here?"

"My dad took me out to get some new shoes and he was coming here so I had to come too. Do you like 'em?"

She held one of her feet aloft so Jonah could see her new white Reeboks. To his dismay, Jonah could also see the missing finger, holding on by the lace.

"Well?"

"Oh. Yeah. Those are . . . real nice."

She really was perfect. And for a few short moments, it didn't matter that three dead fingers were about to beat the shit out of him. He just felt happy to be near her and flattered by such a disarmingly open show of affection. Proudly, he began stomping again.

"Well, Jonah, I gotta go."

"Oh. Okay. I'll see you."

"Yeah, see you."

"Hey, maybe we could go see a movie sometime," said Jonah.

"Okay."

"Next Saturday?"

"Sure, Saturday's good."

They were all smiles.

"Good."

"Good."

"See you later."

"See ya."

Sara left in one direction and, Jonah noticed, the fingers were leaving in the other, sickened no doubt by all this syrupy young love.

*

"Hey, Mr. Burnett?"

"Hey, Jonah. You forget something?"

"No. I was just wondering . . . can I have some sawdust?" Jonah gestured toward the pile beneath the saw.

"Boy, you as crazy . . . hell, I don't care. Take as much as you want."

"I only need a handful."

Luther burst into laughter and walked away, shaking his head and repeating Jonah's last statement to himself. Jonah, grinning in spite of himself, went to the pile, excused himself around the dead guy in the plaid workshirt who was methodically searching the sawdust, and grabbed a handful.

*

Jonah waited at the curb, guarding their purchases while his mom brought the car around. He was ready for trouble. Hoping for trouble. And sure enough, it wasn't long before a ghost sauntered up and lifted his hospital gown to show Jonah the incision in his chest, clamped open with retractors, from which all of his insides were conspicuously absent. Jonah wanted to puke, but threw his handful of sawdust instead and watched the ghost mellow instantly, like an old tabby high on catnip. It was beautiful. He rolled his eyes back to right-side-out, let go of his lifted garment, and sat down cross-legged on the pavement to play with the stuff.

"Jonah, honestly."

Jonah turned around and saw his mother staring at him, hands on her hips. She'd shown up just in time to see him throw a handful of sawdust at nothing.

*

"Ten o'clock, Jonah."

Jonah stood up, turned off the television, and marched straight toward the stairs.

"Jonah, wait!"

He turned and looked at his mother, but said nothing.

"You're not even going to put up a fight?"

"Please can I stay up and watch *ER*, please?"

"That was pathetic."

"Sorry." Jonah started up the steps.

"No kiss?"

Jonah went to his mother, bracing himself against the squeaking wicker as he leaned in and kissed her.

"'Night."

"'Night."

That taken care of, Jonah commenced the task of dragging himself up the stairs.

*

Jonah took off his T-shirt, dropped it without looking, and sat on the end of his bed, head down, skinny shoulders slumped over his rounded, childish belly. He was exhausted.

But he didn't feel like sleeping. He sat there, fighting it—dozing, then reawakening. He kicked his shoes off, undid his belt buckle, and opened his eyes as wide as they would go, then dozed off again.

"What's the matter, kid, can't sleep?"

Jonah awoke with a start and saw his dad.

"I mean, really, son, is this any kind of a way to treat your old man?"

Despite the huge, gaping gash in his neck, he looked great: hair combed straight back, square jaw freshly shaven, suit hanging suavely from his broad shoulders over thin hips. Jonah was overjoyed, and terrified out of his mind.

"Okay, okay, I admit, it's a lot to swallow. But Jonah, I'll tell you this: what's happening is not that I'm here; what's happening is that you can see me."

"But . . ." Jonah began. He was cut off immediately by a knock on his door. He turned away from his dad and before he could say anything, his mother walked right in.

"Jonah, I've been thinking." She was looking at the floor like she did when she was about to roll out lengthy rationale. "You're getting older and it's time that you started making some of your own decisions about things. So, I've decided that if you want to stay up later a few nights a week to watch certain programs, that's fine. With me. Jonah? Are you okay?"

Jonah looked back to his dad, but he was gone.

*

DOWN IN FLAMES

SUSAN SIPPED HER COFFEE IN THE DARKNESS. Sitting alone in the back row of the small screening room, legs crossed, top leg rocking, she watched the film pivot on an edit and move on. "*. . . doing your part to keep Appomattox Technologies active in today's competitive markets. The vial for your urine test . . .*" Susan watched the scene, then allowed her attention to follow the shaft of colored light back to where she could see it as it moved through the plate of glass directly above her. She watched the colors shift for a few moments, then let her head return her attention forward. In front of her she could see the clients, the older one who seemed to have seniority flanked on either side by two younger ones. She studied their haircuts until the audio called her attention back to the screen, where she watched another edit.

*

The film ended and the clients stood up to congratulate the producer, Don.

"First rate . . ."

"Really, top-notch . . ."

"Just the ticket . . ."

"Well, guys, thanks . . ." Don herded the gaggle toward the exit with arm motions and smiles. "With a company like yours it's easy to . . ."

Don found Susan's eye and smiled, twirling his mustache. His outfit, faded jeans and workshirt, cowboy boots and spotty beard, made her smile back. Maybe he thought he was in the Eagles.

"Thanks, Susan. That was perfect."

Of course it was, she thought.

"Thanks," she said.

*

Susan had known that she wanted to be a film editor for as long as she could remember knowing that such an occupation existed. It played into her sense of order. Running the same scene over and over again, slicing out bits until it suited her—really, what could be better? And where else would her brand of sangfroid, her penchant for meticulous precision, and her need for total control be not only tolerated, but sought after? Like vacuuming while the house was clean instead of waiting for it to get dirty, or insisting that she and her son practice fire drills in their own home, it just made sense to her. Locked away in her tiny editing room, windowless and dark, she concentrated to the point where focus obliterated time, and lost herself somewhere between where her fingers worked the keyboard and her eyes met the screen. In her journal entries, typed into the laptop at sixty words per minute after Jonah went to bed, she decided that the loss of self-conciousness and the second-to-second decision-making combined to transform her into pure will, a sensation she valued deeply. When she learned the trade, they were still using razor blades to cut actual celluloid, and the thrill of physically slicing her way through someone else's work was something she'd had to go far to replace.

*

The two boys squatted in the dark, listening for sounds through the wall.

"*Hey Jonah,*" Ross whispered, "*I . . . oops!*"

He lost his grip on his Coke can and it hit the rafters with a loud thud.

"*Ross! They'll hear us!*" Jonah hissed.

"What?" Ross opened his bag of Doritos and began crunching noisily.

"*Jesus fucking Christ, Ross!*"

"What?" Ross wiped the pink strands of insulation from his soda, then opened it. Coke went spraying everywhere.

"*Shhhhh!*"

"What?"

"*You are so stupid . . .*" Jonah whispered.

"I am not . . ." Ross spoke in his regular speaking voice.

Jonah made a silent, grimacing "*Shh!*" with his finger in front of his mouth. On the other side of the wall, the conversation picked up again. The boys fell silent.

"Yeah, he's okay."

"Great buns."

"Totally."

There was laughter all around.

"So come on . . ." Even through the wall the voice was clearly Ross's sister Jocelyn. ". . . tell the truth. Who's your ultimate guy?"

"In the world?"

"Or in school?"

Voice One was Debbie Charles. Voice Two was Andrea Sievert. They were rumored to be lesbians, but Jonah was beginning to doubt it.

"In school."

Both boys leaned in closer.

"Well," said Debbie, "there's this guy. I don't know if you know him. His name's Jonah Hart. He's the cutest."

"You know who I like?" said Andrea. "Your brother, Ross."

The boys looked at each other, stunned. Each could believe it about himself, but neither could believe it about the other. Jonah looked down and began to imagine the difficulties of making out with Debbie, who was a full foot and a half taller than he. Ross's hand strayed involuntarily to his groin.

"We know you're in there, you little shits! Mom! They're in there again!"

Mrs. Hand materialized at the opening to the crawl space and started yelling. The Hands were always yelling. "Ross, get outta there right now! I mean it! Do you hear . . ."

"It's not my fault! We were cleaning! Jocelyn has a diaphragm!" Ross defended himself in bold non sequitur. Jonah closed his eyes and leaned back against the drywall.

*

One of the reasons Ross and Jonah were such good buddies was because they both had dead dads. Ross's dad had died in a bus plunge in India where he had been on assignment for a travel magazine, covering, of all things, bus plunges. Both boys had been in Mr. Haig's third grade class at the time and had bonded immediately.

The Hand family's tragedy was compounded by the fact that some film discovered on the body got shipped back to the magazine, developed, and found to be an entire roll of Mr. Hand cavorting with New Delhi prostitutes. As editors and assistants passed the buck, the prints came to reside amongst the writer's personal effects which were sent directly to Mrs. Hand. She should have known all along that her husband was one of the habitually unfaithful—everyone else did—but she'd spent many years thwarting just the kind of instincts Susan had been developing. She was so devastated by the revelation that she didn't even tell her kids. It didn't matter, they already knew.

*

"'Night, Mom."

"Jonah, could you come here a minute? I'd like to talk to you."

Jonah made his way back down the stairs slowly, racking his brain, trying to figure out what it was that he'd done this time. Susan, sitting in her big chair with her legs crossed, watched her son drag himself across the carpet.

"Is there anything you'd like to tell me?"

Quite obviously, he was going to have to tell her something; and he was pretty sure she'd found the pack of cigarettes in the pocket of his jean jacket. He'd come home late for dinner and flung his jacket on the banister. During dinner, when his mother got up to take a call, she moved it to the hall closet and gave him a small lecture on cleaning up after himself. But she didn't mention the cigarettes, so he figured he'd gotten away with it.

"I'm sorry, Mom. I know you said I shouldn't smoke, but I've only been taking drags and . . ."

"You smoke?"

Jonah groaned.

"Jonah, I can't believe you're smoking! Didn't the X-rays I showed you have any effect? It's bad enough . . ."

Jonah hung his head, wondering why he hadn't just kept his mouth shut.

". . . but we'll have another talk on that later. What I'm concerned about is a phone call I received from your counselor, Mr. Segretti. He said you've been late for your first period class every day this year. Is that true?"

Jonah couldn't see any way out of it. "Yes."

"Jonah? Why?"

"Because every day after homeroom, I smoke on the playground with Paul Bruckner and some of his friends and it makes me late for history."

Paul Bruckner was a true juvenile delinquent. He'd failed so many grades that he could legally drive to junior high school, though occasionally it turned out the cars were stolen. Besides being bad and dumb, Bruckner was also a bully, and the implication was that he was forcing Jonah to smoke.

"Well, what are we going to do about this?"

"Well, I'm not going to smoke anymore, that's for sure," Jonah said, leaping to whatever role the lie required.

His mother, sitting in judgment, thought about that for a few moments.

"You know, Jonah, in life, a lot of people will try to make you do things . . ."

Advice. It indicated the final gauntlet. Jonah assumed a posture of penitence and waited.

". . . boys like that. So really, you might as well start being your own man now. Am I right?"

"Yes."

"Okay then, I'm just going to forget about Mr. Segretti's phone call. Now, what are you going to do tomorrow morning?"

"Start being my own man?"

"That's my boy. Now, kiss your mother and go to bed."

Susan reached out to embrace her son and Jonah caught wind of the slight, sour coffee funk that his mother got from time to time. It was the faintest scent, but it made Jonah suddenly sad and ashamed of his lie. There was only the light from Susan's lamp, the motion of her top leg rocking, and his figure standing before his mother at the end of another long day. She pulled him close to her and Jonah did not pull away. He felt sorry for her.

*

In the dark, alone with the smell of his bed, Jonah became progressively more relaxed until the feeling of being submerged in warm water came over him and he abandoned himself to the sensation. The bright, porcelain whiteness around the edges made the feeling much like that of dozing in the tub, but soon the gleaming would fade and he'd find himself far from the edge, captured by the current and carried off down a warm, wide river. When the current sped up a little, he unhooked, came back into awareness, and looked down at his sleeping body.

*

Jonah looked down at himself—distinct, but not distinct at all—for all the thoughts he'd ever have, including the ones he was having right now, were born of the soul sleeping beneath him. Like looking into a mirror, it provided him the privilege and comfort of actually seeing who he was, only in this case he was looking at himself the way you would a lover as he slept beside you, breathing slowly.

The effect of this should not be understated; above things is such a peaceful place to be. And Jonah's vision was absolute. He looked down at his room and marveled at how every twig related perfectly to the whole of his nest, perched securely in the boughs of his house.

Jonah thought about the roof—and in that instant, he was there. He looked out over his neighborhood and saw how it was all the same nest: an extension of his house, which was an extension of his room, which was an extension of him. He looked down at the world and received the same validation he felt looking down at himself. There was no difference. Which was the thought he woke up with and carried with him into the bathroom. There is no difference between me and this water that I am making yellow with my pee.

*

Susan looked up from her video monitor to see Don's head in her doorway.

"Hi Don, come on in."

Don strutted into the room, preening before he spoke. "Well, they loved it," he said.

"Sit down."

"Oh. Thanks."

Susan had arranged her office so that her worktable was

predominant and anyone who spoke to her had to do so across her desk. And, since she sat on a stool when she worked, she also sat taller that anyone who came to be seated in front of her. This in spite of her diminutive stature.

"So they're pleased."

"Oh, yeah, they love it . . . you did a great job, Susan."

Susan smiled; she knew she had done a great job. Don, the yuppie desperado, cast sideways glances, inclined slightly forward so that she could see where his hair thinned at the top of his head. He had recently replaced his contact lenses with spare, wire frames that made him look ascetic on some days, drab on others; this was a faithful representation: Don *was* ascetic on some days, drab on others.

He'd come into Susan's office to ask her out. Susan had known he was going to for a few weeks now. And now, here he was. Susan was enjoying herself.

"So listen . . ."

Susan sat, perched high atop her stool.

". . . I was wondering . . ."

Her expression feigned polite confusion.

". . . if you'd like to go out sometime, you know, get some dinner, see a movie or something."

Susan paused to consider before she spoke.

"Don, have you ever been sued for sexual harassment?"

*

"Don, I was kidding . . ."

Don was trying his best not to be irate, but he'd just seen his career flash in front of his eyes. "Jesus Christ, Susan, you shouldn't kid about a thing like that. I mean, that's . . ."

Susan waited until he had finished. "So, you still want to take me out?"

"Not if you're going to sue me."

"Don, I was kidding."

"You know, Susan, you really shouldn't . . ." Don repeated, but then caught himself. "Saturday good?" he said instead.

"Saturday's good. Eight o'clock?"

"Yeah, sure." Don looked around as if he were seeing the room for the first time. It was unadorned, windowless, empty except for this small woman, her machines, and her tools. "Let me know when you think of something you'd like to do," he said.

Susan smiled. Don looked around the room again, then wandered out the door.

*

Jonah sat at the foot of his bed, sound asleep and fully dressed, abdomen slowly expanding and contracting as his breath distilled itself into the air of the room. Unconscious, he existed as a force of nature: a tulip in the moonlight. Each inhalation built him up and then broke him like a wave upon the beach.

An expression washed across Jonah's features. He moved his head slightly and let out a sentence and a half of gibberish.

"What's that you say?"

Jonah opened his eyes and looked up at his dad, dumbstruck.

"Hey, kid, speak to me. How you doing?"

"Um, fine."

Dan looked at him like he doubted it. Outside, the first truly cold night of the season was frosting Jonah's windowpanes. The wind was blowing, but all the leaves were gone from the trees so there was no sound to it.

"How's your mom?"

"She's . . ." Jonah said, but even as he answered a question came to his lips. "Haven't you seen her?"

Dan sighed, bubbles appearing in the blood at the edges of the gash in his neck. "Nope," he finally said.

"Why not?"

"Beats me. I guess I don't exist for her."

Jonah swallowed and closed his eyes. He could hear the wind now, blowing against the windowpane with a soft, rushing roar. "Can you remember her?"

"Memories, son, are for those still alive. I don't exist for her, therefore she doesn't exist for me."

"I don't get it."

"There's nothing to get. Or, I can't explain it. Words, Jonah, we're using words. I'm a ghost. I don't like to get caught up in such temporary agreements." Dan brought out a martini, which he sipped genteelly, leaning forward so the clear fluid wouldn't stain his suit as it dripped from his injury.

Jonah watched, utterly confused. "Does that mean you exist only in my imagination?"

"Shit!" Dan exclaimed as his foot passed through a pile of laundry he was trying to kick. "I exist only in my son's imagination. Shit!"

Jonah was crestfallen. "Then I'm crazy," he concluded.

Dan flashed a show-biz smile. "I'll show you crazy," he said. He measured three steps back, one to the side, and with a deft, soccer-style kick, sent Jonah's Washington Redskins trash can flying across the room.

*

Jonah waited for Sara on the bench beneath the big clock at the Overston Mills Mall, looking at his shoes. He'd arrived for their date an hour early and was exhausted from glancing up every two minutes to see if it was her.

"Hey man, it doesn't have to be this way."

Jonah looked up and saw an athletic middle-aged man with a clipboard, eyeing him intensely and offering him a flyer that had "*1-800-RUNAWAY*" printed in large type across the bottom. Jonah laughed, relieved the guy wasn't a ghost.

"Oh, thanks, I'm . . . I live at home. With my mom."

The man wasn't buying it. "Take the material, man. It doesn't have to be this way."

Jonah took the flyer and went back to looking at his shoes. Twin escalators on either side of him carried shoppers to the level below and thin winter sunlight streamed in from skylights in the vaulted ceilings. The sound of conversation and movement echoed off every surface. Jonah slouched, oblivious.

*

Milliseconds before Sara plunked herself down on the bench next to Jonah, he caught scent of her creme rinse and looked up.

"Hi, Jonah!" She smiled at him widely. Her knee touched his thigh, and she made no attempt to move it. Jonah felt electrified.

"Hi!" Jonah returned her smile with such total lack of self-consciousness it was a miracle he didn't drool. They smiled for a while, looking each other in the eyes.

"Am I late?"

"No, I was . . . early."

"Bummer for you." Sara's knee remained locked on target.

"Oh, but, I had to get here early. To meet some people." Jonah smiled and relaxed just a notch. "Business associates."

Sara's laugh sparkled like a birdsong. "Yeah, right . . ."

Jonah lowered his voice a register. "There's much you don't know about me, Sara Benson."

He was flirting boldly. The smell of creme rinse had driven him mad.

*

In front of the marquis at the movie theater, they licked their ice-cream cones and debated their choices.

"What about *Receptor?*"

"Nah. That's so fake. Droids can't mate with humans."

"Well, what about *Voyage Quest?*"

"That on a submarine?"

"I thought it was a spaceship."

"We could see *Doodads.*"

"Isn't that for kids?"

Jonah entertained vague feelings of embarrassment. Was it wrong to want to see a kid's movie?

They reviewed the remaining titles in silence.

*

In the end, they opted for *Shotgun Party*, reasoning that, since the advertising played up both its humor and the violence, there was a greater chance they'd be entertained. And they were. They ate all of their popcorn and candy in the first five minutes and laughed at every joke, all smiles and glad to be there.

*

Jonah located the phone on the fifth ring.

"Hello?"

"Jonah. Ross."

"Hey, Ross."

"I can't believe you didn't tell me."

"Tell you what?"

"Dude, don't play innocent. You know very well *what.*"

Ross was always undergoing a crisis of some sort, and Jonah, who had spread himself out on the bed, decided to indulge him. Because it was Sunday, because there was nothing he had to do, and above all, because this morning he just felt kinda happy. "Ross. Really. I don't know what you're talking about. Really."

"I'm just shocked you wouldn't tell me, that's all."

"Tell you what, Ross?"

"We're best friends, aren't we?"

"Yeah, but . . ."

"Best friends tell each other everything, right?"

"Yeah, but . . ."

"I can't believe you didn't tell me, Jonah!"

"Tell you what?!"

Jonah waited calmly while his friend's anger diffused into silence. "Sara Benson, Jonah. Sara Benson!"

"Oh yeah . . ."

"I can't believe you didn't . . ."

His date with Sara really had slipped his mind, but it certainly did explain this morning's good mood. Ross expounded on topics like trust and betrayal. Jonah stretched out where he lay and let the particulars of last night's date flood back into his mind.

"Jonah?"

"What?"

"*What.* Didn't you hear any of what I've been saying? You know, friends are supposed to . . ."

*

Ross paused and Jonah began paying attention again.

"So. You gonna tell me what happened?"

"Sure, if you shut up for a minute."

"Do you hear me talking?"

"Yeah, I do."

"Jonah, goddammit . . ."

Jonah laughed. The way Ross swore made him sound like an angry clergyman.

"Okay, okay. We went to a movie . . ."

Jonah recounted the details.

"And then?"

"What?"

"*What.* Jonah, I swear, you are so dense. How far did you get?"

"Oh, well, I . . ."

Jonah stammered, trying to figure out what to say. He wasn't exactly sure what was expected of him. He was, however, sure that "I forgot to try" was not the right answer.

"Goddammit, Ross, that's none of your business." It was Jonah's turn to sound like an angry preacher. Ross laughed.

"I knew it. Nada. Zero. Crash and burn. Down in flames, dude. You blew it."

"Did not!"

"Totally did. Hmm. I thought she liked you . . ."

"She does!"

"Then why'd she burn you like that?"

"She didn't . . . I didn't . . . even try."

"You didn't even try? What are you, a fag?"

Jonah felt like he was standing in a hole. Ten minutes ago he'd been on top of the world without a clue as to why. Now, he knew the reason and was totally bummed. Ross was busily explaining What Girls Really Want, a thing boys learn at around age fifteen and suffer from for the rest of their lives. Jonah couldn't listen. He was thinking about the skinny ghost.

After the movie, he and Sara had gone into a record store. The ghost had been in the section devoted to 12" dance singles, moving his emaciated body in rhythm to the BPMs. Jonah would have guessed that he had starved to death somewhere, only he was still wearing his hospital gown, and people don't starve to death in hospitals. He was balding and had a thick, well-kept mustache, and when he had noticed that Jonah could see him, he had narrowed his eyes to slits and mouthed the words, *"Give. Me. A. Kiss."*

A chill ran down Jonah's spine just remembering it. Ross was still talking and Jonah went back to listening.

". . . like, is there something wrong with her?"

"No way! She's great."

"So then what's your problem, Jonah?"

"I don't know, I . . ."

"You're going to have to ask her out again, as soon as possible."

"I'm gonna."

"Yeah, but this time you're going to have to make a move."

"But . . ."

"Right. I'm coming over and we'll figure out what you're going to do. We've got to move fast. You know what I'm saying?"

"But . . ."

"Okay. See you."

"But . . ."

"Bye."

Jonah hung up and pulled the covers over his head. With his head in darkness and the bright noontime sun warming the backs of his legs, he slept until Ross came over.

*

Ross and Jonah were agreed. Hart would call subject at exactly 19:30 hours on Wednesday, October 31, 1990. Hart would ascertain subject's willingness to view another movie, and if said willingness was forthcoming, subject would be encouraged to visit Hart's residence where the two would view the film via videocassette. In this fashion, Hart would be in control of all variables: seating, music, lighting, potential use of alcohol, et cetera, and more importantly, between 19:00 and 23:00 hours, Hart's mom would be on a date with some loser she worked with and he'd have the house to himself.

At the video store, the two boys relied upon the expertise of Gibby, who was their favorite clerk due to his pronounced "short front/long back" hairstyle and his willingness to let them browse the Adult section. According to Gib, all seduction boiled down to three basic scenarios, and it was decided that when the time came, Sara would be allowed to choose between *Nine and a Half Weeks*, the story of a short-term, sadomasochistic love-a-thon; *Blue Lagoon*, a film where a boy and girl grow up alone on a tropical island and have to figure out what they're going to do with all the hormones; and *When Harry Met Sally*, wherein a man and a woman become friends first, then do it. Regardless of which film the subject chose, the outcome was certain: The Gibster guaranteed it.

*

Fresh from the shower, Jonah combed his hair, examined the effect in the mirror and, dissatisfied, messed it up and tried again. He looked at his reflection with a frown, then got back into the shower and started over.

The day was not going well. His morning oatmeal had been too hot and he'd burned his tongue on the first spoonful, so everything since had tasted like scar tissue. He had strained his shoulder carrying wood to the car at the hardware store and now couldn't lift his arm without pain. But mostly, it was the ghosts. Lots of them.

He looked in the mirror, still dissatisfied, and decided to do what he always did—towel dry the stuff and leave his poor head alone. He wrapped the towel around his bony hips, passed behind the ghost who was on her hands and knees cleaning the tub, and made his way to his bedroom.

Since Jonah had no mirrors in his room, he had to travel to the full-length mirror in his mother's room to judge his different outfits. The trip took him past the window at the front of the house that overlooked their street by which Susan had placed a marble-topped Victorian bathing table along with a big pitcher and a washing bowl filled with potpourri. Today the arrangement included a ghost, and every time Jonah went from the first door to the third, the man in the funeral suit would take the pitcher, slowly invert it, and look at Jonah as if to say, *"See? There's nothing in here."* The few times Jonah let his glance rest too long, the dead man smiled and winked. Only when ghosts smile, it's more like they're showing you their teeth. And when they wink, the eyelid is the only part of the face that moves. It goes up and down like a window shade.

It would be difficult to say whether Jonah finally settled on the perfect outfit or just got tired of changing, but he ended up going with his Air Jordans, jeans, and a white, long-sleeved T-shirt with a breast pocket. Finally prepared, he went downstairs and sat at the kitchen table. Sara was due to arrive at 7:30 p.m. Jonah checked his watch. That gave him exactly four hours and thirty-seven minutes. Jonah looked at the ghost who liked to stand in the sink. When he caught her eye, she smiled and winked. Jonah sighed and put his forehead on the table.

It hurt his nose to have it squished flat on the table like that, but it seemed somehow appropriate and so he did not move. After ten minutes he noticed that he had to piss and he didn't even feel like doing that. He just sat there, feeling the pressure against his bladder, thinking of Sara and how unconcerned she probably was about the evening. The comparison chafed, so he thought instead about how he was going to make his move, but vague anxiety drove those thoughts away. He finally just sat there and wondered when he was going to get up and piss. The ghost in the sink began to march in place, her footfalls ringing in light cadence against the stainless steel. The sound had no physicality; there was neither attack nor echo.

*

Eventually, he went to the bathroom, and when he flushed, six gallons of water carried his cup or so of urine out of his house and into the sewer system where it could play with the other wastes of the neighborhood in a river that you could not imagine even in the pits of your worst nightmares. Like a watershed, it starts with what rains down from above, trickling into creeks which join to form rivers which meet in bays and inlets to feed the sea. In the darkness beneath the pavement runs the stuff you don't want to see even long enough to throw away—the shit, piss, and vomit of millions that surges along with all of those six-gallon flushes, and there's more, toenails, hair, ashes, tampons, cigarettes, dental floss, toilet paper, and worse: animals, digits, fetuses. Filth.

*

Jonah checked his hair while the toilet refilled its tank and as soon as they were both finished, he headed back downstairs. Once in the kitchen he opened the refrigerator and looked for a long time, noticing brand names and finally opting for a Coke, which he poured over ice with a slice of lime. He would have sat on the sofa and maybe even watched TV, but there were two old dead ladies already there. They wore opaque eyeglasses with thick, black frames and formless floral print dresses, and the only way Jonah could tell where their legs ended and the orthopedic shoes began was by the change in color. One of them was knitting something, but it looked like a dead animal, so Jonah didn't look too closely. He stood there with his glass and his can, unsure of his next move. They looked at him, then at each other, and laughed raucously at some private joke. No waves carried the sound to his ears. He heard only his synapses, firing reflexively in anticipation of sound that never came.

*

When the doorbell rang, Jonah sprung away from his image in the bathroom mirror and hurried downstairs to answer the door, but paused in his descent to do a quick double check. His right hand shot across his chest, where it reassured itself with the soft weight of the sawdust in the breast pocket; his left hand dropped to his jeans where it fingered the circular form of a condom beneath the denim.

*

Jonah flung the door open. Sara stood on the threshold, smiling.
   "Hi."
   "Hi."
   That was all they could muster for the moment. Darkness had fallen, the low red clouds were reflecting the street lights of the city, and their breath was escaping them in billowing streams of condensation. Jonah couldn't believe how pretty she was.
   "Can I come in?"
   "Oh. Yeah. Yeah yeah yeah, come in, come in."
   He stood aside so she could pass, and her proximity sent a rush of blood to his ears.
   "Thanks."
   "You're welcome."
   They stood in the front hallway and Jonah, hands in pockets, took his best shot at nonchalance.
   "So. How are you?"
   "Fine. Maybe you should shut the door."
   "Oh."
   Once she was safely inside, Jonah began to remember his manners.

"Can I take your coat?"

"Umm, I'm not wearing one."

"Oh. You must be cold."

"No, I'm inside now."

"Oh. Do you want to sit down?"

"Okay."

Sara walked into the living room. Jonah panicked instantly. Were the dead ladies still on the sofa?

"Jonah?"

Jonah answered on his way to the kitchen: "I'm getting something to drink," he yelled. "You want something?"

"Whatcha got?" Sara yelled back.

Jonah opened the refrigerator and recited at the top of his lungs: "SPRING WATER, SELTZER WATER, ORANGE JUICE, DIET COKE, MILK, BEER, AND WINE!" He emphasized the last two.

"ORANGE JUICE!" shouted Sara.

Jonah, on the verge of shouting "OKAY!" checked himself. He had suddenly noticed a dozen little dead girls in blood-spattered leotards holding a conference around the kitchen table, and it now took all the concentration he had to pour two glasses of O.J. The girl at the head of the table nearest Jonah gestured in presentation, but all she had for materials were two pieces of bread and an oven mitt.

Jonah sighed. The whole house had become a haven for spirits. There was a dead cleaning lady in the bathroom, a dead guy with a pitcher in the upstairs hallway, a dead marching lady in the kitchen sink, a whole flock of little dead girls around the kitchen table, and, when he carried the drinks in to Sara, he confirmed it, two old dead ladies in the living room. They were squinched up against one another on the left side of the sofa, right next to Sara, who was sitting on the cushion in the middle. Jonah handed her her drink, set his on the right arm of the couch, then went to the stereo to put on some music that Ross guaranteed would put Sara "in the mood."

"I didn't know you liked classical music."

Jonah sensed admiration in Sara's voice and preened accordingly.

"Oh, yeah, some of it's really good."

"What's this?"

"Bo-lair-o," Jonah said, looking at the album cover as he sat down next to her.

"It's nice."

She smiled at him. Could Ross have been right? They sat there for a little while, Sara looking around and Jonah drinking his juice like he was searching it for clues.

*

Sara spoke first.

"Have you started your science report yet?"

"Sort of."

"Sort of? What's your topic?"

"Extraterrestrials: They Walk Among Us."

"You're kidding. Colson said you could do that?"

"Not exactly. But Ross's mom's new boyfriend bought him a video camera, so we're going to do our own *Alien Autopsy*." Grinning, Jonah added, "We're using a Purdue Oven Stuffer Roaster with an alien mask for a head."

Sara cackled and punched him on his sore arm. "That's great! Ha!" The old ladies rubbed their arms and pantomimed the word, *"Ow."* Jonah stole a glance at his watch and saw that it was already 20:00 hours.

"Your mom sure does have a lot of books."

"Want to watch the movie?"

"Oh. Okay, sure. Whatcha get?"

"You pick."

Jonah brought the movies over. Sara was nonplussed by the odd variety and chose *Nine and a Half Weeks* because she figured maybe it was an Action/Adventure film. Jonah became agitated because the film had sadomasochistic sex scenes in it and Gib had said that if she chose it, it meant she wanted it bad. His hands trembled as he shoved the thing in the VCR.

"Oh, wait a minute. Want some snacks?"

"Okay."

Jonah hit the pause button and the FBI warning against unauthorized use flickered on the screen.

*

He walked slowly toward the kitchen, giving the little dead girls who had been eavesdropping in the doorway a chance to clear out. They did, returning in a cluster to the kitchen table. There were more of them now, some of them horribly mutilated. Though it was a feeling he had rather than an actual sound, it seemed to Jonah that they were all laughing, and that the laughter was like leaves rustling in the wind, leaves the color of their leotards—pastels and whites. Jonah looked at the one closest to him, with a stoved-in head and blotches of crimson across her top. She smiled and winked. And then they were all winking and the sound was that of butterflies fluttering. He finished as quickly as he could and returned to the living room carrying a Tray of Many Snacks, prepared six hours ago, which he placed on the coffee table.

"Wow, Jonah, this is great."

It was. There were crackers, cheese, grapes, quartered cucumbers, and more, all calculated to look like the kind of thing adults would serve and thus make Jonah seem worldly. Sara and Jonah dove into the big bowl of Cool Ranch–flavored Doritos and washed their handfuls down with big slurps of juice.

"What are those?"

"Smoked oysters. Want some?"

"You like those things?"

"Oh yeah, they're great." Jonah slathered a bunch on a cracker and popped it in his mouth. He'd never eaten oysters before and was shocked at what an unbelievably nasty foodstuff they were.

"Help yourself," he managed to say.

Jonah, holding the food in his mouth so that it touched as little of his tongue as possible, unpaused the movie, clicked off the lights, and sat back down, sliding in a little closer to Sara. While the opening credits rolled, he made a series of careful swallows and washed the whole unpleasantness down with the last of his juice.

*

The action was moving at a glacial pace and Jonah, whose mind had wandered off, found himself back in the moment. On-screen, the pas de deux of seduction and domination slowly unfolded, punctuated occasionally by explosive fucking. Cast in an eighties sensibility and steeped in psychological nuance, the whole thing shot right over the heads of the two children on the couch. Jonah looked over to Sara and instead saw the two old ladies, who were now sitting in between them. How had that happened? They smiled chummily at him, and he glared back.

Sara looked up to find the expression aimed at her. "What are you looking at me like that for?" Her question had an unmistakable undertone of disdain.

Jonah peered at her, dismayed. Moments ago they'd been on the verge of nestling; now she was at the opposite end of the couch, her arms wrapped around her legs and her nose touching her knees. "I, umm . . ." His mind geared reflexively toward a plausible explanation, but none came.

On-screen, Kim Basinger flew into a rage at Mickey Rourke, who responded by wrestling her onto the dining room table and nailing her. She enjoyed it and Sara and Jonah each settled into a separate, silent confusion.

The real dilemma though, was that according to plan, Jonah was supposed to put his arm around her now. It was quite obvious that now was not the time, but Jonah was having a hard time balancing his conflicting urges. The two old ladies had gotten up, one now mounting the other on Susan's ottoman, and Jonah made his move, only he had forgotten about his strained arm and when he raised it up and slid toward Sara, the pain that struck like lightning in the center of his shoulder caused him to moan audibly.

"Jonah. *What* are you doing?"

*

Jonah had developed a certain doggedness in the face of humiliation, one which was now so practiced that it could masquerade as grace under pressure, and here in the face of doom it allowed him to laugh. Which was the only possible thing he could possibly have done to save himself. It was a laugh of naturalness and resignation and it disarmed Sara, who was beginning to wonder if maybe she shouldn't leave. On-screen, Kim Basinger was in the country with an old man who seemed to be a new character. Sara returned her attention to the movie, but not before giving Jonah a look that said, "*I got my eye on you, Bucko.*" Jonah slumped back on the sofa and began sucking ice cubes. This made Sara feel better too. Jonah always slumped, even when he was standing. It had been disconcerting the way he'd been perching.

*

The movie ended and the credits ended and the tape ran out and the VCR clicked off and the TV started hissing at them.

"So . . ."

"Yeah."

"Whew."

"I know."

"I can't believe Gibby liked that one."

"Who's Gibby?"

"The guy at Potomac Video with tattoos on his hands."

"Ooh, he's creepy."

"Yeah, he practically made us . . . *me* get it."

"That's really weird."

"Yeah."

Jonah looked over and saw the old ladies in postcoital recline, smoking and nuzzling.

"This is a nice sofa."

"Me and my mom just reupholstered it."

"Really?"

"Oh yeah, it was easy . . ."

Jonah saw his chance. As he referred to the sofa while describing the details of fixing it up, it was only natural for him to place his arm along the top and pat it for emphasis. But to avoid pain, he didn't so much place his arm up there as fling it like a prosthesis. It was a weird thing to have done, but as far as he could tell, it hadn't spoiled the mood. And it left his arm one step closer to Sara's shoulders.

"How did you know how to do it?"

"My mom buys these instructional videos. We built those shelves too." While pointing to the shelves with his left arm, he eased his right closer to Sara.

"You did?"

"Oh yeah, you just go to the hardware store and . . ."

One of the old ladies moved onto the far arm of the sofa and both began giving the V for Victory sign the way Winston Churchill did,

tonguing the web of skin between the two fingers, and moaning ever
so slightly.

"Jonah, are you okay?"

"Oh, yeah, where was I?"

"Knotty pine."

"That's right. So, anyway . . ."

Sara was looking at him funny, and though he realized that it was
a weird thing to do, he looked down at the floor so as not to be
distracted by the old ladies' obscene gestures.

". . . so that even though it took up three weekends, if was really
only like ten hours of work."

"Wow, that's really great."

Jonah looked up, smiling, but had to put his head back down
immediately because the old ladies were sticking their middle
fingers through circles made with their thumbs and index fingers
and leering while they nodded in approval.

Jonah didn't think he could take much more of this.

*

"What other projects are you gonna do?"

Jonah, enduring extreme shoulder pain as he reached into his
breast pocket and pulled out a handful of sawdust, missed the
question. He placed the dust on the back of the sofa and flicked it at
the ghosts, who didn't notice at first; they were busy French-kissing.

"Jonah, what are you doing?"

Jonah didn't say anything. He just watched her as she got up,
marveling at how much he liked her. The two ladies had gone for
the sawdust and were playfully rubbing it in each other's hair.

"I think I'd better go."

Jonah smiled, but found himself on the verge of tears and erased
all expression from his face.

"Bye, okay?"

Jonah nodded and looked away. Moments later he heard the front
door close.

*

Jonah sat on the sofa with his eyes shut, listening to the sounds around him. The old ladies were arguing, but their words lacked definition, like conversation heard through a wall. In the kitchen, the little girls swished and fluttered while their giggles hung in the air. He could hear the rasp of the cleaning lady scraping her brush across the tub and the clank of the man with the vase as he slammed the object rhythmically upon the marble-topped table. I am insane, Jonah thought. Driven by the clang of tin upon stone, the wash of sound grew structured and became a song, growing louder inside his head. The scraping became polyrhythm, the giggles accented like horns, and the argument turned into melody, a song stuck inside Jonah's head, which, try as he might, he couldn't shake. It got louder and louder, and Jonah, about to cry out, put his hands to his ears in a vain attempt to block the noise. The volume split his brain like a headache and he stiffened against the pain, which become more and more unbearable as the sound increased in intensity, until he couldn't take it anymore and screamed with all his might. That instant, the noise and the pain vanished and the scream died, half-formed, in his throat. He opened his eyes and looked up. The house was empty.

*

Jonah yawned and stretched. Suddenly, he felt very sleepy.

*

TINY SUICIDE

SARA'S ROOM HAD BEEN REMOVED INTACT and installed in their new house when her father won his research grant and they moved from their farmhouse in Iowa. The simple walnut bed, shelves, and desk—her prized possessions—had been her mother's as a girl. She painted the walls pastel blue, just like they'd been at home, and compensated for the lack of animals by covering her walls with posters of them.

"Hi, Mrs. Wannamaker. Is Sandra there?"

Sara relaxed on her bed, cradling the cordless phone between her shoulder and ear. She pulled her wet hair back into a ponytail, which she secured with the rubber band from her wrist, then drew her right leg up to her lap and ran her fingers along its smooth, freshly shaved surface.

"Hello?"

"Hey, Sandra."

"Hey yourself."

Sara lay back on the mattress and let her fingers trail down her sternum to the flat muscles along her abdomen.

"Is there something you guys aren't telling me about Jonah?"

"What do you mean?"

"Is there, like, something wrong with him?"

"Well, he's short, but I don't think that . . ."

"I don't care about that. But . . . why does he get so weird?"

"Oh, that."

"*That?* You mean it's a *that?*"

"No, no, well, sort of. Jonah's just weird, that's all. Did he remember to try and kiss you this time?"

"Yeah, but I wouldn't let him." Sara straightened her robe and pulled the sash taut around her waist.

"But you said . . ."

"I know what I said. I changed my mind."

"You changed your mind? Don't you like him anymore?"

"Of course I do. I just don't . . ." Sara let the sentence fall short. "Don't" seemed to cover it.

*

Sara couldn't put her finger on it, but she knew: There was something wrong with Jonah. In Iowa, she'd adopted a dog they found living in the barn that must have been abused by its former owner because it took Sara all summer just to get it to take food from her hand. After countless hours spent encouraging the dog to suffer her presence, he eventually allowed her to pet him, but the look in his eye as he trembled beneath her touch came to mind as she considered Jonah.

"Sandra, can you hang on? The other line's beeping."

Sara clicked over. "Hello?"

"Um, is Sara there?"

"This is she."

"Oh, hey Sara, it's Bobby."

"Hi, Bobby, hold on a second . . . Sandra, ohmygod, Bobby Brockman's on the other line."

"Bobby Brockman! Okay, but you have to call me when you're through talking or I swear to God . . ."

Sara didn't wait for her friend to finish. "Hi, Bobby. How are you?"

*

Jonah opened his eyes. The red LED numerals of his clock radio read 2:56 a.m. Sitting on the edge of his bed in his underwear, he sighed and slumped forward.

"You're alone, chief. She doesn't need you anymore."

Jonah turned sharply and looked at his dad. "What are you talking about?"

Dan rolled his eyes sarcastically and looked away, silently repeating the question. "Who do you think I'm talking about?"

Jonah looked at his bare feet, dangling.

"That's right, I'm talking about Sara."

Dan straightened his tie and took a sip from his drink while he waited for a response. He was dressed immaculately, as always:

three-piece suit, silk tie, starched cuffs, diamond cufflinks. Jonah pouted and Dan continued. "She doesn't need you. She's not the new kid anymore. Your mother didn't need me, either. It's a man's lot in life. In the end, you'll find yourself alone. Don't worry. Hell, you'll find lots of girls if that's what you want. You'll have lots of friends too if you want 'em. But in the end, you're alone."

"What do *you* know? You're dead."

"Am I?"

"Aren't you?"

"You're talking to me. I'm alive somewhere."

Jonah responded tangentially: "But you're an alcoholic."

"Jonah. Honestly. I drank a little bit too much . . ."

"I can't believe it. You're still in denial."

Dan looked at his drink and swirled the liquid. "Yes, I suppose I am. But life is hard. As you well know." Dan grinned winningly at his son. "Tell me. What's the difference between my drinking and your dreaming?"

*

Jonah found himself standing speechless before his father. Or the apparition of his father. He couldn't be sure. The lamp from the small bedside table cast a half-light about the room and his head swam in the hollow of time that forms the wee hours of the morning.

"What . . . what do you mean?"

"I mean to suggest that the apple doesn't fall too far from the tree." Dan leaned forward and sipped his drink.

"Get out of here!"

Dan laughed. "Words must have meaning, son, if they're to have any effect."

"I mean it. Get out of here!"

"But you don't mean it, kid. That's the problem." Dan reached forward and put his hand on his son's face, preparing to give him a push. It didn't happen. Jonah had fallen asleep.

*

When Jonah went dreaming, he was like a fish. His disembodied consciousness darted slowly here and there, adjusting his position within the current that carried him along. He thought about the roof and suddenly found himself there, looking down at moldering shingles and up at geomagnetism, linking the two with whatever it was he had become. He set his heart on the tops of the trees that grew in the park at the end of his street and felt himself drawn to them.

A full moon with a fat ring around it arced across the sky and, noting the brightness of its light, Jonah wondered what it would be like to sleep all day and float beneath the penetrating rays of the sun. Could he do that? He drifted along, musing, with no particular notion of where he was until he saw headlights approaching. The light was thin and pale, illuminating objects caught in its beam, but without brightness. When the car pulled up in front of his house, he recognized it as his mother's and watched her park and get out.

"Hey, mom," he said.

But the words were thoughts; there was no sound.

*

Susan passed beneath him and he wondered momentarily if he should follow her in. Usually wondering if he should do a thing was enough to get him headed toward it, but this time it didn't happen. Jonah continued to float toward the trees.

*

It was 1:00 a.m. when Susan arrived home from her date. Walking up the steps, she hummed happily to herself. She'd made a good choice in Don; everything was going to work out fine.

In reviewing *The Movie That Was Her Life*, Susan had highlighted a need for companionship and embarked upon a methodical search. She finally settled upon Don, who, in her estimation, was sensitive enough to not be domineering, self-made enough to be interesting, easily amused, not bad looking, and, since he'd been divorced three times, cured of any romantic illusions. She lured him by laughing at his jokes, holding his glances, and commenting favorably on his outfits, and had reeled him in over the course of their long evening together. Her thought, as she worked the key in the front door of her house in the dark and quiet of a frozen winter's morning, was that men were an awful lot like trout.

They'd gone bowling. Don resisted at first, especially when Susan insisted that she drive, but once he got it into his brain that he wasn't going to be able to impress her with his new BMW or his knowledge of French wines, he loosened up. Susan beat the pants off him. On the various army bases of her youth, she'd killed endless hours in bowling alleys and Don, who hadn't bowled since some half-remembered thirteenth birthday party, never stood a chance. Susan, for whom the fun had started when she saw Don, the powerful producer, sitting on his hands in the passenger seat, proved quite the bubbly woman. Much to Don's delight, she talked openly about herself, laughing loudly at her own self-deprecatory jokes. It was the tone of the entire evening—unguarded, silly. Don responded in kind.

Susan secured all the locks behind her, turned off the porch light, and examined the darkened downstairs. The full moon lit the inside of her house and she could distinctly see her library, her chair, and the table next to it, where her laptop had gone to sleep and her cup of coffee had gone cold. Her eyes lost their focus as she stood in the entryway and worried vaguely about Jonah. He'd been incommunicative lately, though now that she thought about it, "lately" had already lasted a year. What can you do when your son stops telling you stuff? He's got a right to privacy like anyone else.

It was the same conclusion she always came to. She felt no need for alarm. Since all adolescents act a little crazy, she'd wait for a warning sign that was impossible to ignore before doing what needed to be done. Susan roused herself and marched into the kitchen, where she poked casually through the garbage, snooping for any evidence Jonah's night adventures might have left and thinking about her evening.

When she and Don had finished their games, they repaired to the bowling alley's Snak Shoppe where they drank Cokes and shared an order of the worst onion rings ever made. It was funny to them, and they ate them anyway, laughing and saying, "These are terrible," and, "Yup, these are terrible alright." When the onion rings were gone, they ordered more Coke which they sipped slowly, gossiping about coworkers and playing occasional footsie.

The whole thing had taken Don pretty much by surprise. His

penchant for diminutive brunettes with long hair and full lips had taken him strange places before, but he could never recall feeling so out of his element while having so much fun. Susan was a marvel; nothing she'd ever done at work had led him to suspect that she could be this goofy. And nothing could have surprised him as much as when Susan, on the way home, drove in the wrong direction to see how long it would take him to notice. Sure it was a bad joke, but he didn't mind; it turned him on to watch her drive. He watched her until they pulled up in front of his house where, for the simple reason that he didn't want the evening to end, he invited her in.

"Next time," was what she'd said.

Don the trout flapped happily in the creel.

*

Susan sat in the darkened hallway chewing the eraser on her pencil while the answering machine rewound. The taste in her mouth was inseparable from the feelings in her heart, feelings of home, security, and order. The feeble creakings of a worn cassette were all that disturbed the stillness, and Susan sat with the taste, the feelings, and the freedom from anxiety that come from absolute union with one's domain. The machine clicked into play and the messages began.

"Hi, Susan, it's Estoban, just calling to say the film looks great, you're a genius. I'm in Miami til Tuesday, I'll call you when I get back. Kisses."
Click.

"Um, hi? This is Lester from the co-op . . . I'm calling to let Susan know that her bulk order of soy milk has arrived and she can come pick it up now . . . um, thanks. Um, bye."
Click.

"Hi, this is Vivian Woods with the counseling staff at Fillmore Jr. High? Just a routine call to let you know that I've posted a list of recommended mental health professionals that we send to our parents whose children are having difficulties and if you have any questions about what kind of therapy would be best please feel free to contact me. Also, so you know, we recommend that our single mothers seek counseling as well, so, again, if you have any questions at all, I can be reached at the school's counseling center during regular business hours. Okay? Thank you."
Click.

Susan found she'd bitten off the end of her eraser.

*

Jonah approached the stand of Norfolk Pine, entranced by what he beheld. At a distance they looked like a mass of shrouded forms, but as he got closer he could see them individually, swaying in the frozen breezes, beckoning with many arms. He tried to hurry toward them, but his pace remained consistent, slow. He drifted among them and spoke, though the sound of his words had no echo, no location.

What are you doing here, trees?

We grew here.

How?

We've always grown here.

The trees were laughing and the sound was the wind through their needles. The wind picked up, and Jonah found refuge within the small thicket.

What does it mean, to be a tree?

Jonah weaved his way through the upper boughs, staying close to the trunk, listening.

None of us is a tree, they were saying. We are all the trees. We turn soil into air.

Jonah stuck the part of himself that he would have referred to as his head into the nearest trunk and felt his consciousness expand immediately through the sap in the tubular cells, up into the sky and down into earth, felt himself flung upward above the soil line and dragged downward below, felt his needles exchanging CO_2 for O_2 and his root hairs moving through the soil, turning its minerals into tree. It's all the same, he was thinking, and, how feeble our distinctions—air, tree, earth. Still his consciousness expanded, to the unlimited potential of the seeds which lay all around, dormant, waiting for spring, to the selfless death of the pines which lay rotting, becoming soil, becoming tree, becoming air, becoming . . .

Jonah pulled his head out.

*

Ow, he thought. I wonder if that hurt.

He wondered about it for a while, then noticed that he'd floated far from the trees. Bye, trees. He floated along, musing, with no particular notion of where he was until, after a while, he looked down and recognized the neighborhood. He was near Sandra's house. An image of his friend, sprawled on her bed with her large breasts fully exposed, presented itself, and Jonah hung himself out upon the air, listening for the beating of Sandra's heart and let the suckings and spittings of its ventricles draw him toward her.

*

The boys paid attention to Sandra because she had big breasts. Though it's a given—boys stare at tits—Sandra had grown increasingly annoyed that they seemed to be holding conversations with her boobs rather than with her, and subsequently was developing a pointed distrust concerning the motives of others. This habitual skepticism became a useful tool and she began to excel academically, refusing to take anything she read or heard at face value. Her ability to routinely cite outside sources endeared her to her teachers and their subsequent willingness to treat her as an equal provided her with the encouragement she needed to drop the ditz routine that had won her praise thus far and pursue an aggressive self-reliance. In law school she would find to her delight that she was able to core anyone else's arguments in short order, and to her dismay that her male peers hadn't changed one bit. Her subsequent crusade against injustice landed her several high-profile anti-bias judgements and, eventually, a judgeship.

Jonah smiled. He'd floated in through the window and was reading the story of her life, evident in the outline of her jaw, the marrow in her bones, and the rise and fall of her mighty chest. He watched her little pink mouth draw breath and could see how she'd get married relatively late in life, to a man she could trust.

*

When Sandra's heart let him go, Jonah floated up to the roof. He was experiencing deep feelings of wholesomeness and acceptance. A phone rang, and the sound pulled him into motion, only it wasn't a phone ringing, it was crickets chirping, but that was impossible because it was winter. It was the power lines humming. Or something. Suspended above the sleeping neighborhood, he did a triple gainer with a half-twist and started to laugh at how silly that was, only right as the laugh was about to burst from his lungs it spread instead from his middle in a series of concentric circles and left him relaxed and forgetful. Where am I? he thought. Then he saw Kim's house.

*

The boys didn't pay much attention to Kim. She had small breasts, she loved reading so much she sometimes brought books to parties, and the knowledge gained during hours spent in study gave her perspective on the things that fifteen-year-olds take so, so seriously. She imagined she had friends—everyone treated her like one of the gang—but she was going through life largely ignored, even by her mother and father. She compensated for the lack of affection by being compulsively neat. Not only was every item in her room dusted, catalogued, and put away perfectly, but for her fifteenth birthday, she asked for and received an ionizer. After all, what's the point of cleaning your room if you're going to fill it with dirty particles?

Jonah floated a millimeter above her. She lay perfectly parallel in her bed, which was squared to the four corners of the room. He wanted to see her find a partner who would love her like Sandra's; instead, he watched her loneliness reach critical mass when she entered graduate school where, deciding to specialize in early American literature, she discovered that the story of her life no longer held any interest. She killed herself in the ladies' room at the library, slowly swallowing forty-three sleeping pills. She chose Impramine because of its low therapeutic index—as little as eight would kill. Typically, and for the last time in her life, she'd done a better job than anyone would care to notice. When they found her, three books lay neatly stacked on the floor at her feet: Kate Chopin's *The Awakening*, Buckminster Fuller's *Critical Path*, and *Little Birds* by Anäis Nin.

Tonight, though, she slept peacefully and Jonah watched her future suicide, apparent in her chest, moving up and down, while the negatively charged ions moved easily in and out of her young, healthy lungs. Jonah could also see that she had a crush on him. An old one. She must have had it for years.

*

83

The dreams just wouldn't end. It seemed to Jonah that he got three or four nights' worth of travel from a single night of dreams. Like right now, as he floated in and out of a soda can in a neighbor's backyard, there was nothing that wasn't interesting, and time didn't seem to matter at all. Still, no matter how far he pushed it, he always made it back to his body in time to wake up in the morning.

*

He returned to his house and floated in as slowly as he could, the flow of his movement barely perceptible, like the lengthening of shadows. Eventually, he found himself in front of his mother's gun case.

His mother had two guns. The Colt Peacemaker, a gift from her daddy, had originally belonged to her great-grandfather, who, Jonah could see, had actually shot people with it. Three deaths lingered at the end of the long, heavy barrel. Jonah could see cloth leaping away from the sudden red dots of entrance wounds, brutish, decisive. Two men and one woman, dead long ago. He could see them gradually coming into focus, but a smell, or what would have been a smell, low and sweet, like the air outside the rendering plant, broke his concentration. Far away, part of him shuddered.

The other gun was a Glock 9mm, black and curvy, with the sensitive five-pound trigger Susan required for her tournaments, where she put holes in paper targets. Thousands and thousands of paper holes. Jonah drifted off.

As he rose to the ceiling he saw the key to the cabinet lying on the top right-hand corner in a small circle cleared in the dust. So that's where she keeps it, Jonah thought. He approached the key, watching it get bigger and bigger. When he finally sidled up to it, it was as big as a battleship. He floated alongside, studying the massive copper contours, thinking: A key exists only to enter and open. Like bullets.

*

Jonah looked down on his mom. Her room was empty except for the huge four-poster bed and its matching cherry vanity, and saw that she was as beautiful as any of the younger women he'd been with that evening. Susan's face looked as if sleep pained her, but while Jonah searched her wrinkles for meaning, he saw only the carefree nature she'd lost along with her childhood. He thought back to midnight feedings and remembered what it was like when his mom was the universe and he'd drawn life directly from her. He noticed an opaque speck on her right breast, studied it momentarily, then returned to his memories, passing through the birth canal and into a world where all sounds were music and all motion was prayer.

*

"So. Would you like to come inside?" Don was cool, confident. She had let him drive this time.

"Sure." Susan smiled.

Each held the other's glance in one of those deliciously anticipatory moments, then separated to let themselves out of Don's sleek black BMW. They'd gone to see *The Seventh Seal* and *Fanny and Alexander* and the experience held meaning for both of them: You can't take just anyone to a Bergman double feature. Don held open the door to his house, and as Susan crossed the threshold, she gasped.

"Wow, Don, nice place."

It was, technically: state-of-the-art audio and video components prominently placed, lots of chrome and glass and angular, low-slung furniture throughout, and on the wall along which one would have expected to find the sofa, an actual Pollock. Don had very definite ideas about how rooms should look, and though he'd never know it, it was the way his living room looked as much as anything else that had driven away each of his three wives. It was unbelievably tacky.

"Really nice," said Susan. "I love Ikea."

Don was aghast. He began to sputter and gestured at the painting, on the verge of saying, "It's a real Pollock . . ." when Susan interrupted.

"Don, I'm kidding."

Don continued to sputter, nevertheless. "That's a $2000 television."

"Don, I know . . ."

"These chairs were originally designed . . ." He was starting to wind down. ". . . imported Italian . . ."

She let him run out of steam. Then, she spoke: "Hey, give me the tour."

Don brightened.

*

Susan followed behind while Don led the way. "This, of course, is the kitchen. The tiles are Italian, there's no way I could afford them if I were to buy them today. I swiped them from my grandfather, actually. He . . ."

". . . originally going to be a circular staircase, though at one point I actually considered an elevator and a fireman's pole . . ."

". . . my office . . ."

". . . the guest room . . ."

Susan listened, but what she heard were not his words, but the inevitability of what was to come. The tour could not help but end in the bedroom. When Don began, Susan followed, neither planning nor imagining what came next. She became a Susan she did not see when reviewing the movie of her life, a Susan who was invisible in retrospect, a Susan vulnerable in the world of things: a Susan who was not in control.

*

Don's room smelled of incense, though Susan didn't notice. She didn't notice how near he held himself as she passed through the doorway, nor did she notice herself walking to the bed and letting her hand trail absently along the linens. She was in waiting.

The breach came sweetly, in the form of a large hand on her shoulder that lingered on the muscle, searching for tension and gently kneading. "My God, Susan, your shoulders are like iron bars."

Susan leaned into Don, who had seated them both on the edge of the bed. She was on the verge of tears; it felt so good to be touched.

*

It's like riding a bike: the best bike you ever had. Susan and Don worked themselves gradually around until they were both in the seat, so to speak, and rode like they'd been doing it their whole lives.

Susan had had a baby, so she knew the risks. Don had had three wives, so he did too. Both of them knew that you could die from it these days, but they'd taken all the obvious precautions and were applying themselves with a carefree diligence that left them panting on their backs, inarticulate.

*

As she lay intertwined with Don, casually inspecting the moles on his chest and enjoying the musty smell they had made, she decided quite resolutely not to spend the night. The intimacy that produced their orgasms had been perfect, a fellowship, a ride through the park. Nice. But sleeping together would be too much. It would ruin everything.

But not yet. She lingered a while in the forgetful aftermath, not thinking about work, not thinking about Jonah, not thinking about anything. Soon, though, her mind returned to the call she'd made that afternoon, to the counselor at Jonah's school. She had listened attentively and said "Yes" and "Uh-huh" at all the appropriate junctures as the counselor went on about the strains on Susan, common to many single mothers, and how it was time to introduce a strong male presence into Jonah's life, if not in the form of a male therapist, then through one of the many fine mentor programs here in town. When she was done, Susan had thanked her, hung up, and looked down at the fresh notepad in her lap on which she'd written not a single word. This is how it replayed in the Movie That Was Susan's Life: a pleasant conversation in which there'd been nothing worth noting.

*

Jonah decided that the only way to both make it to Erlichmann's class on time and avoid the ghost with no trousers would be to hang out in homeroom until the last possible moment, then run as fast as he could all the way there. He'd told Ross about Mr. Segretti's phone call, figuring Ross would start blabbing immediately. If everyone knew he had to make it to class on time or else, no one would think it too unusual if they saw him running through the halls like he'd seen a ghost. It seemed the perfect solution.

"Tony Garcia?"

"Here."

"Jenny Grant?"

"Here."

"Jonah Hart?"

Pause.

"Jonah Hart."

"Oh. Here."

Jonah's homeroom teacher, Mr. Halderman, gave him a look that said, *"Don't take that tone with me, young man,"* and moved on. "Tammy Hoyt?"

Jonah glanced up at the clock. Five past. In five minutes, he'd have five minutes to make it to Erlichmann's class. He figured it would probably take one minute and thirty seconds running at top speed and barring any mishaps. He looked at his watch which corroborated the testimony of the wall clock. Six past.

"Jonah?"

"Yes, sir?"

"Does your leg have any particular reason to be going up and down like that?"

"Oh. Um, no. Sorry."

*

"Okay, people, I'm handing out your schedules for yearbook pictures. You'll notice that the times are assigned according to the first letter of your last name, so make sure to note your day, and on that day you'll go to the armory instead of homeroom. Clear?"

Jonah noted that his day wasn't for several weeks and stopped paying attention. Since their names were Hart and Hand, he and Ross would be next to each other in line anyway and Ross would probably remember what to do when the time came. Besides, it was T minus two minutes and counting and Jonah was concentrating on how to stall until it was time to dash.

*

The bell rang and the room erupted into the kinetic lethargy of kids on their way to class. Halderman spoke over the din of the shuffling. "Jonah? Can I talk to you a minute?"

"Yes, sir."

"What does Erlichmann think?"

"He doesn't like it."

"He's told you this?"

"Yes, sir."

"Okay." He looked up at the clock. "You'd better get going."

Jonah turned to go.

"Oh, Jonah?"

"Yes, sir?"

"If this continues, you're going to have to see Liddy."

"Yes, sir."

If Jonah hadn't been determined to get to class on time before, he was now. Everyone was afraid of Principal Liddy.

*

In the hallway outside his homeroom, Jonah warmed up by running in place and shaking his arms loose while the first of the morning's stragglers hurried toward the classrooms around him. He knelt down to tighten the laces of his basketball shoes, otherwise casually unstrung, and, still kneeling, looked at his watch. Four. Three. Two. One. *Go.*

He thrust himself up out of his crouch like a racer out of the blocks. At the first corner, as he moved out of shadow and into the brightness of the main hallway, he passed a group of girls clustered around a locker. One of them yelled, "Go Jonah!" and the rest of them giggled. Well done, Ross.

Halfway across the hall, he zagged into the stairwell and skittered back and forth down the stairs, his padded footfalls reverberating against the marble and into the huge space that had opened above him. At the bottom, he hit the doors with a bang, veered right, and lengthened his stride for the long straight sprint that would take him down the front hallway and into the New Wing. He leaned forward into his pace, pulling his big shoes along behind him, and when he reached the end of the hall, he took all eight steps in a single bound. It occurred to Jonah that he ought to be seeing the ghost right about now, but he didn't want to think about that, so he let the thought go. A dozen long strides took him to the door of his classroom where he screeched to a halt and walked on in. He peered up at the clock.

Three seconds to spare. Jonah looked over at Erlichmann, who was looking back at him with genuine surprise.

"Well. Will wonders never cease."

*

Out of breath and the center of attention, Jonah collected himself and made his way to his seat. He could see Sara, seated at the desk behind his, searching for something in her notebook.

"Hi, Sara," he said, but she didn't look up. He faced her for a moment more, then sat down, and placed his head on his desk.

*

SIX-PACK

SPRING WAS COMING. Jonah could see it clearly, especially when he dreamed at night. He was dreaming now, only it was the middle of the day, and the sun's shimmering rays made everything seem underwater. Objects were no less distinct than they were at night, but they appeared to be buoyed up, waving slowly in the current. After he and his mom had put a final coat of paint on the kitchen cabinets, he excused himself, crawled into bed, and submerged. And though this wasn't the first time he'd done his dream traveling during the day, he was hard put to remember when he had done it before. Dreaming during the day was different. He'd just hang out in his room, like you would at the bottom of a swimming pool if you could breathe underwater, then wander outside, where he was hanging now, watching the weeds rip the pavement to shreds.

*

Ross would have been the quarterback, but cold rains had left the field too slick to do much running.

"I'm just tired of it, that's all!" Ross said, slinging the ball up in an easy arc. Jonah fielded it absently.

"Well, how many boyfriends does she have?"

Ross rolled his eyes up and to the right in mental calculation. "Nine. That we know about."

Jonah smiled and Ross became suspicious. "What. You think it's funny my mom has nine boyfriends?"

"No. Not at all. Your mother is a very attractive woman . . ."

Ross held onto the ball he'd just caught and rested it on his hip, indignant.

"Oh yeah? Well your mom is . . . so . . . um . . ."

*

Ross was big. It was just one of the things that made Jonah and Ross such an odd pair, but it struck you immediately; Ross was really big. And although Ross was not dumb, he wasn't quick, and since a big dumb guy teamed up with a small smart guy is an American archetype, not only did teachers and friends relate to Ross as the big dumb guy, but sometimes Jonah did too.

Ross ran out of steam searching for a retort and resorted to a legitimate question.

"Well, how come your mom doesn't have any?"

"She has one. I think."

"You think?"

They began to throw the ball back and forth again.

"Well, I know he's her boyfriend 'cause every time she talks about him she calls him, 'my friend, Don . . .'"

Ross laughed. Jonah's impression of his mother was uncanny.

". . . but he's never around, you know. I mean, in the morning."

"You're lucky. My mom's boyfriends are always around in the morning, eating all our food and telling me what to do."

Jonah thought about Don trying to behave like his dad. The image was not unappealing and Jonah found himself suddenly sad.

*

"You know," continued Ross, "your mom is like the head of the CIA."

"Oh yeah? Well your mom spreads like Jif."

Ross fell immediately silent. He'd meant that Susan compartmentalized information, keeping track of who knew what and telling people only what they needed to know. Jonah's retort smacked of anger, and Ross didn't know what to do.

So he threw the ball. Only as he released it, he found that he'd put all of his strength into the throw. It hit Jonah in the chest and knocked him flat on his butt in the wet grass.

*

Jonah was forcing corncobs down the garbage disposal when his mother called to him from the living room. "Jonah, could you come here for a minute? I'd like to talk to you."

He tossed the cobs in the garbage and grabbed the towel that hung from the handle of the refrigerator door. As far as he could remember, he really hadn't done anything worth getting mad at since he'd been grounded for sticking opened Oreos on Don's BMW two months ago. The filling ate through the paint and Don just about flipped.

"I'm coming," he called back.

He approached her chair and waited.

"Jonah, have you had any more of those stomachaches?"

"No. No, they've pretty much gone away."

"Well, I want you to see a doctor anyway. I called Dr. Hess and made an appointment for you to see him next Thursday."

"Awww, Mom . . ."

"Jonah, we made a deal."

"I know, but I'm okay, really, I'm okay."

"So there'll be no problem having a doctor tell us that too."

"Mom . . ."

"Jonah . . ."

Jonah exhaled in exasperation. "But Mom, I'm fine."

"Good."

"Mom . . ."

Susan mocked her son in a playful tenor. "*Mom . . .*" she sang.

"But I'm fine."

She held her arm out in an operatic gesture and sang the words, "*But I'm fine!*"

"Goddammit . . ."

Susan laughed when her son swore, stuck her fingers in her cooled tea and flicked them at Jonah. Jonah exhaled sharply and stomped off.

*

"What are you looking at?"

Jonah, sitting sidesaddle on the radiator at the window, yawned and turned to greet his dad. "Oh, hey Dad," he said, and returned his attention to the house next door. Dan came up behind him, to see what he saw.

"Hey yourself. Who's that?"

"I think that's the guy who hung himself before we lived in this neighborhood."

They watched the man, strung by the neck from the dining room chandelier, grinning and using his legs to move back and forth like a kid on a swing set. Dan scratched at the edge of his neck wound as if it itched. No scabs had formed; he had yet to stop bleeding.

"Dad, can I ask you a question?"

"Fire away." Dan moved without walking to the middle of the bedroom, glowing a faint red and illuminating the pile of dirty clothes at the foot of the bed. Dan sipped his cocktail and Jonah, frowning, spoke his mind.

"Is this it? Am I always going to be like this?"

"Jonah, just because I'm dead doesn't mean I can see the future. After all . . ."

Jonah exploded. "Can't you just give me a straight answer? Is that too much to ask?"

"Jonah, I'm hearing a lot of anger."

Jonah rolled his eyes and said, "You're fuckin' right you're hearing a lot of anger! This sucks! What am I going to tell that fucking doctor?"

When Dan next spoke, Jonah felt his father's voice whispering simultaneously in both his ears. As he turned toward the sound, he found his father gone. In his place, the room glowed a deep, flickering red. *"Okay, kid, you want straight, I'll give you straight. It's up to you. It's your problem. Your mess to clean."* The words buzzed closely in his head, neck, and chest, bringing an uncomfortable warmth to those areas. *"Solve your problems,"* the words said. *"Make decisions."*

The words, or the voice that carried them, disappeared and Jonah felt his skin cooling. The room slowly darkened and Jonah looked back at the hanged man who twisted slowly, feet twitching in quick, spastic motion.

*

That evening Jonah thought about the doctor's appointment as he soaked in the bathwater that would eventually carry him to his dreams. He tried on story after story, but each gave way to the belief that doctors knew everything and therefore, if you were to lie effectively, you had to know everything too. Which Jonah didn't.

He decided to stop thinking and go dreaming instead, so he

floated downstream, unhooked, and came back into consciousness looking down at himself. He hung there for a while, watching waste move through his intestines.

From there he wandered outside, carried by the ringing of a telephone, which Jonah experienced as a tingling as it lifted him out of his room and down to the front lawn, where he stared at the crab grass and dandelions mixed in with Kentucky Bluegrass and Turftype Fescue that he and his mother had sown many Saturdays ago. It had been easy. Just toss the shit around and it grows.

*

When the phone stopped ringing, Jonah felt like the engines had been cut and he was now drifting. Not a bad feeling at all. Jonah felt buoyant and lucky. He floated along just above the grass, conscious now of the microorganisms rippling the soil, and watched the grasses waft lazily in the current. He thought he saw a quarter over by the gas meter and tried to breaststroke over to it, but nothing happened. He just continued on toward what he could only call his left.

The current picked up and he was carried along; as the speed gradually increased Jonah felt that he was being pulled toward something. Unable to alter his course, he just floated along with it.

*

How many hours had he been here? Jonah examined the inside of the Coke can with fascinated awe. I love you, Coke can, Jonah thought, and then giggled.

The longer he hung out in the dreamscape, the more he noticed that a hole of any kind behaved like a vortex, a whirlpool convergence of flow that would draw him in. He'd been floating down an alley and the can had just kinda sucked him in. He didn't mind. Not really. One place was much the same as the next. *I have seen the best Coke cans of my generation* . . . Jonah started, but then lost himself.

*

Jonah stretched, but nothing happened. Or if it did, it was back where his body lay sleeping in the bed. He wondered about it and then didn't. It wasn't important.

*

Hello, Sara. Jonah was circling in the air up by the ceiling of her room. It blew his mind. He kept ending up in the most interesting places.

Sara and Jonah had not been on speaking terms since Sara, who harbored a lingering fondness for Jonah, cashed out of her "new kid" position to put a down payment on popularity. Jonah, increasingly tangential to his circle of friends and fighting to maintain his composure, became increasingly sullen and withdrawn. And easier to ignore.

From his vantage point just under the ceiling, Jonah watched Sara distance herself as if it were a TV show visible on her closed eyes.

Goodbye, Sara, he thought.

*

It was getting close to the time when he would have to wake up. He didn't know this for certain, but the events of his odyssey had evolved to the point where a return to his body felt imminent. It never failed. At some point during the night, he'd round a corner and find himself home.

Jonah ended the night in his own basement where the rising sun filled the room with an illuminated, underwater blue. Jonah swam lazily over to the windows above the utility sink, whose bars were shimmering amidst the UV rays, then circled the series of iron posts, entering each and feeling how the house rested on it. He rose up within the last one and continued through the staircase on the first floor and into midair on the second. Between floors, he could see the whole house filling with blue. It poured through all the windows, finding its way under doors and through cracks, dripping from the railings and banisters.

*

Before he rejoined himself in bed, he stopped to look at Susan. She made a habit of sleeping with the curtains pulled wide so that the sunrise would wake her before her alarms and the light lit her like an X-ray. Jonah could see the outline of her skeleton and all of her internal organs, her sleeping face troubled as it squinted, eyes closed, against the light that was about to wake her. Of particular interest today was her womb, busily purging itself of its former lining. He could also still see the speck at the corner of her left breast. It had grown in definition and it looked like a set of plastic six-pack rings.

*

Jonah awoke to the dawning realization that he felt awful. His mouth was dry, his eyes felt stuck in their sockets, and, when he rolled from one position to another, flashes of pain struck the sides of his skull.

"Ohhh . . ." Jonah moaned. What day was it? The weekend, he hoped. The thought of having to leave the warm confines of his sheets seemed more than he could bear. He supposed he should at least look to see what time it was.

"Jonah! Time to wake up!"

Jonah screamed and bolted upright in bed. The man with the pitcher, who had just yelled directly into his face, turned and walked away. He didn't seem mad at all. Just doing his job. Jonah dragged himself out of bed and into the bathroom to face the day.

*

"Hand!"

"Hart! How you doing?"

Jonah and Ross always referred to each other by their surnames when they were forced to line up alphabetically.

"You look sharp, man."

"Thanks. You look pretty good yourself."

"Thanks."

They were grinning like maniacs. Jonah wore a shirt with fat red and white vertical stripes that he'd picked up at a thrift store and a paisley bow tie that he'd saved out of his dad's stuff before his mom gave it all to Goodwill. Ross wore a T-shirt with a photo of a pair of breasts, positioned so as to be anatomically accurate, which he'd bought at the beach the summer before. Both boys had styled their hair back and up for a wind-tunnel/mad-scientist effect.

"I love yearbook photos. Don't you?"

"Yes, yes I do."

Their grins intensified as each looked at the other and they both began to giggle helplessly.

"You look so dumb."

"I know. So do you."

"I know."

Now completely convulsed with laughter, the two boys barely managed to shuffle along with the line of students that led to the guy who worked the camera.

"What if they don't let us wear this stuff?" Jonah asked.

"They will," Ross said. "I've got insurance."

"Insurance? What are you talking about?"

"You'll see."

Last year they'd worn afro wigs. The plan had been that while the photo was being taken, Ross would lean as far as he could to his left and Jonah would lean as far as he could to his right, so that when the yearbook came out, they'd look like Siamese twins joined at the head, only the guy taking the photos had refused to let them do it. This time, though, Ross's air of certainty was so convincing that it put any doubts Jonah had to rest and the two of them took advantage of the time away from class to pinch, snicker, and generally behave like geeks.

"Tell me this, Hart. Why *do* people smile for photographs?"

"I don't know, Hand. Why do people smile for photographs?"

"No, I'm serious."

"I don't know. You're just supposed to."

"But why?"

"I don't know. Maybe so when you look back, it'll seem like you were happy."

"Think so?"

"I don't know."

"Then from now on, dude, I'm only gonna smile for photos if I really feel like it. I mean, why would you want to lie to yourself?"

Jonah wasn't really listening. He'd just caught a whiff of something fetid and was busy wondering what it could be.

An added bonus of lining up alphabetically was that it put Martha Hanby and the Hancock twins in front of them. Amy and Ann Hancock were admired from afar by everyone because they were identical, because they modeled, and because they only dated college guys. Ross had a crush on Martha; she also bore a striking resemblance to his mom, though Ross denied this vigorously.

The girls all wore dresses, and once the boys got tired of bickering, they fell to staring at the girls' legs in silent, open-mouthed fascination.

*

When their turn came, Ross sprang into action. The school had decided on the photographer's "Rural Romance" package, so in addition to a picture of a barn with some trees next to it, there was a plastic mock-up of a hand-hewn, split-rail fence on which they were encouraged to either cross their arms or fold their hands. Just as Ann Hancock started leaving the set, distraught and asking her sister, "But why, Amy, why? Why would they want it to look as if we're in an animal pen?" Ross sidled up to the cameraman, a balding, middle-aged man with a shiny forehead, and put a twenty-dollar bill into his palm with both hands.

"My friend and I would be very disappointed if, for some reason, we weren't able to have our pictures taken today. Do you understand what I'm saying?"

Jonah didn't catch the man's reaction, but he did see Ross's triumphant thumbs-up, as his friend took his place inside the pen. In position, Ross checked to make sure he actually felt happy, realized he did, and smiled wide, his chest stretching the breasts on his T-shirt, making him look like the proudest hermaphrodite in the world.

*

Ross pulled his friend out of his reverie.

"Jonah, your turn. Jonah!"

Jonah moved slowly to take his place. The stench was growing in intensity. "What's that smell?"

"*Jonah*," Ross hissed between his teeth, "I just paid twenty bucks for this. Don't fuck it up, okay?"

"Okay. Sure."

"Keep your eye on the birdy," the camera guy said. He actually had a rubber chicken, suspended by a rope from one of the camera's appendages.

"Do it," said Ross, walking backwards off the set.

Jonah walked into place, looked back at the line of students waiting their turn, and saw what smelled so bad.

*

It was Bobby Hartman. He'd drowned the summer before, inner tubing on the river fed by the waterfall. It had been a large group of boys and girls, floating and joking, and because their cooler full of sodas wouldn't cooperate by floating along with them, Bobby had tied it to his leg with the cord from one of the rafts. The summer had been drier than usual so the river ran low, exposing the snags that they otherwise would have drifted right over. Ten minutes before they reached the boathouse where one of their mothers waited, Bobby spilled out of his tube, and the ice chest got hooked in the snag that had spilled him. He was a good swimmer, but caught like that, he was unable to escape the current that held him down. His crew floated happily on, noticing his absence only after they'd returned to shore. Park rangers found the body quickly—the red cooler sat high in the snag, barely touching the water and clearly visible. The death shook everyone up, but by the time school started, Jonah had forgotten about it. Bobby had forgotten about it too, for there he was, standing in line, waiting to have his picture taken like everybody else.

Jonah positioned himself in front of the camera, beginning to gag. It smelled so bad Jonah thought his DNA might unwind.

*

Bobby looked like they'd never found him, his skin pinkish and gray like clay mixed with too much water. Naked and featureless, his whole body wobbled in its efforts to stay upright. He took a step forward, dragging the cooler along behind him, and his head, or at least the hairy lump of flesh that passed for a head, lolled all the way backwards off his shoulders and disappeared from view. Jonah's lower jaw dropped and his forehead rose, creating a camera face much better than any he could have produced on purpose. The shutter clicked and Jonah's attention turned to the dark spots the flash left inside his eyes. Ross came up and led him away.

"That was beautiful, Jonah, really beautiful. Best twenty bucks I ever spent."

*

"Don, why did your third wife leave you?"

Don was now accustomed to Susan's abrupt manner. Not only was he no longer taken aback, he found it endearing. "Not an easy question to answer. There's a long version and a short version. And her version and my version."

"Start with the simple and then work toward the more complex."

"Okay. Simply put, I don't believe marriage is a personal debt . . ."

It was a beautiful spring Saturday, and Susan and Don were walking along the C&O Canal, holding hands. ". . . to change according to their expectations of . . ."

Susan sensed something hidden about Don, a depth to his character unexplained by the surface facts of his life. She'd tasted it on his tongue the first night she slept with him, and had been trying to track it down ever since. Her question was only the most recent in a long line of questions, strung out over the last few months, that she was calmly, methodically using to winnow out the secret.

". . . and make a lot of money. And I come from money, you know, and for people who've never . . ."

When they reached a grassy area suitably shady for their picnic, Susan made for it and Don, still talking, followed.

". . . my idea of . . . oh, yes, this will do nicely . . . or should I say her idea of . . ."

*

They made a nice couple: Susan liked to listen and Don liked to talk. Don continued as Susan prepared the picnic around them.

". . . of course, I did refuse to be flexible about the living room, but . . ."

They'd stopped at a fast food take-out chicken place and gotten

Don a four-piece assortment that included cole slaw, french fries, biscuits, and a large soft drink. Susan had packed a tofu salad on a bed of fresh greens with lemon-ginger dressing, a loaf of freshly baked whole wheat bread, and a box of fruit-juice-sweetened cookies of which Don was highly suspicious. She spread the big pink blanket next to a great tree and opened and arranged the various cardboard and tupperware containers until they were surrounded by food.

Susan's efficiency belied the warmth of the day around her. Cyclists rolled by, other couples and families with children wandered amidst the sudden, blooming green, happy and relaxed, while Susan placed and sorted, the small muscles of her sleeveless arms rippling with her efforts, her concentration locked on what Don was saying. "Wait a minute. Go back. What would your first wife say when you'd do that?"

"Well, it was different with Donna, she was my first love and we'd . . ."

*

In his profession, Don was expected to talk all the time, and he'd developed the ability to use words to postpone meaning and create the illusion that he knew much more about a topic than whoever was listening. It was easy; he was the boss. Unfortunately, years ago, he'd forgotten that it was just a strategy that he'd built for times when he didn't have much to say, and he started talking that way all the time. Which is to say Don tended to go on and on.

Susan, on the other hand, knew precisely what was on her mind at all times and if called to, would simply state it. The challenge for her lay in mapping the wilds behind the eyes of others. Her critical listening skills and intuition, informed by a handful of continuing education classes in psycholinguistics, allowed her to hone in on the structure of a thought made manifest in words; Susan often felt she knew more about how people felt than they did. "Go back, go back. None of that was an issue for your first wife. Why'd you guys split, anyway? Here, eat."

Don retrieved a drumstick from the greasy paper basket she offered him. Susan wiped her hands with a napkin and gnawed on a piece of bread.

"Could we talk about something else?"

"Sure, babe. How's the chicken?"

"Good," Don said. Chewing, he looked at the meat, while his face formed an expression usually reserved for something that tastes bad.

*

After their meal, Don became incommunicative and grouchy, but Susan had read all about that; guys feel like they lose status when they discuss their problems, so if something's really on their mind, they'll clam up. Susan stopped prying and Don eased his head down into her lap and promptly fell asleep.

Sleepy men, she thought. Jonah was still sleeping when she had left the house at 11:00 a.m. The kid sure could sleep.

Don mumbled something from his dream. Susan, lost in thought, didn't hear it.

*

For some reason, his father was wearing sunglasses.

Jonah stood at the center of his bed, testing the weight of a cardboard poster tube which he then held behind him at the ready. His father, atop a pitcher's mound of dirty clothes, shook his head in response to signals from an imaginary catcher. Finally, he nodded and hurled the rolled-up sock they were using as a ball. Jonah swung and missed.

"Steeeeeeeeeee-rike one!" Dan grinned beneath the silver lenses of his aviators. Jonah spoke quietly in response, imagining Susan working in her chair downstairs. It didn't matter how loud his dad yelled, but he had to remember to keep his own voice down.

"Come on, Dad, give it all you got."

Jonah caught a piece of the next pitch, but it flew foul off the bat and disappeared behind the chest of drawers. Dan carefully rolled a new one and went into his crouch. He wound up and let the ball fly. Jonah stood helplessly as the pitch went wild and smacked him on the side of his face.

He woke with a start to an empty room. He turned to his clock, red digits standing out against the darkness. It was five o'clock in the morning.

*

It seemed to Jonah as if he had been dreaming for weeks. He couldn't remember ever having wandered for this long; still, he felt nothing compelling him to return. He floated in and out of the cross sections of the jungle gym at the elementary school in full daylight, watching how the thousands of young hands and feet had worn the paint away, how the wood chips below were being ground into soil, and, judging from the streaks of pain left behind on the bars, how dangerous this toy was. He moved from streak to streak, examining the imprints left by tiny craniums, shins, and elbows.

No one was around and Jonah wondered why there was no school today. He discovered a small jacket, discarded in the bushes, and wandered along the weave of the cloth, following it in and out, in and out. It just kept on going.

*

Jonah floated, approximately fifty feet above the deserted playground, watching the sun go down. When the day turned the corner on evening, Jonah noticed the difference in the play of shadows, and it slowly dawned on him that the playground was empty because it was Saturday. Saturday day. Morning had come, but his dream had continued, and now it was night again.

Jonah stretched himself out on the cool night air. Oh well, he thought.

*

Susan sat on Jonah's bed, watching his sleeping body and feeling vaguely troubled. After her nap with Don, which to their surprise had lasted two hours, she became increasingly concerned about Jonah, and called home several times, from the restaurant, the theater, and Don's bedside phone, but all she got was her own voice on the machine. She looked around the room without seeing, waiting for the inner voice that usually spoke so clearly, but it was not cooperating.

"Jonah, honey . . ."

Susan gave him a little nudge between his shoulder blades but he didn't respond. Something was wrong. For the first time in her life, she didn't know what it was.

*

Her date with Don had ended on a slightly uncomfortable note. For as long as they'd been dating, Susan grilled him about the facts of his life and came to know, in that way she had, that Don was hiding something. As she fit the larger pieces together, she began concentrating on the events surrounding his first marriage. He and his first wife had been very much in love and were having, as far as Susan could tell, a perfect life together. Particularly intriguing was Don's tendency to reminisce happily about the particulars of their time together and then get a pained, faraway expression on his face.

When their lovemaking ended a question popped into Susan's mind.

"Why didn't you have any kids?" she asked.

"We did," Don responded. "Twin girls."

"She got custody?"

Don was silent for a full minute before he responded.

"They died," he said. "They were coming home from ballet class with a vanload of their little friends and got run off the road by a drunk driver.

"They died," he repeated. "All of them."

*

Outside homeroom, Jonah stretched as he did every morning, getting ready for his dash to first period. He rubbed at the corners of his eyes which were itchy from pollen, looked at his watch—what the heck, close enough—and started. Not up from a crouch, but with long easy strides, biding his time until he found his pace. It was a warm spring day outside and everyone walked a little slower, relaxing, as Jonah wove his way around those remaining in the hallway. Outside the windows, an explosion of green signalled the turning of the season. Jonah ran lazily, thinking of other things. He hadn't seen the janitor for weeks.

Someone had opened the windows along the front hallway of the now-deserted first floor and the air came straight in off the grass, fresh and damp. As Jonah pulled it into his lungs, it relaxed him so much that he didn't even panic when he saw the ghost.

The janitor was at the bottom of the steps leading to the New Wing, looking wistfully out an open window and leaning against the sill, arms crossed, his bare flanks to Jonah. The boy slowed. When he drew even with the dead janitor, he stopped and waited, slightly out of breath. The janitor turned, saw him, then turned back, uninterested. Jonah called to him: "Hey, ghost."

"Fuck you," the ghost replied, not turning around.

"Seriously. I've got a question."

"Scram. Asshole."

Even as Jonah spoke the words, he wondered to himself why on earth he was doing this. He felt like Eve, chatting with the snake. He looked around, made sure they were alone, then continued. "How come you're not chasing me?"

"Cocksucker. Dick."

"Look at me."

Much to his surprise, the ghost complied. He reminded Jonah of his friends who were getting very drunk at parties these days: stupefied, belligerent, and quite helpless.

"Pussy."

"Why aren't you chasing me?"

"Butt-boy. Fag."

"Why aren't you chasing me?"

"Fucker . . ."

"Tell me!"

". . . douche bag . . ."

"Fuck you, then."

The ghost began to laugh. He laughed so hard that at the end of each breath, he fell into helpless coughing fits. He put his face to the window, steadying himself with his arm on the sill, and pulled in huge lungfuls of air which, it seemed to Jonah, had him high as a kite. "Hee-heee!" (Cough, cough) "Geek! Ninny! Guinea! Haaah-haaah . . ."

The ghost fell to the ground and lay there in a wheezing, giggling heap. Finally, bored, Jonah went to class. More confused than ever.

*

Jonah would not see the dead janitor again until the fall. Ghost season was ending, retreating with the advance of the warm weather, though a few lingered here and there: the one he figured was his grandfather who followed his mom around sometimes, the dead lady with the nice smile who stayed by the macaroni and cheese in the supermarket, and, of course, the fingers in the hardware store. But even they were subdued, and sometimes appeared as little more than flickers.

*

"So. What seems to be the problem?" Dr. Hess rubbed his dry pink hands together with a faint, sandpaper-on-wood sound while he looked at Jonah's chart over the top of his glasses.

"Stomachaches."

"Hmmmm . . ." Dr. Hess frowned at the chart. Jonah wondered if he had somehow given a wrong answer. Still, when the doctor looked up, his face softened into a smile. The lenses of the doctor's glasses magnified his eyes slightly, so that despite the friendly demeanor, Jonah felt on edge. The way anyone would when preparing to lie through their teeth to an expert.

"How often do they occur?"

"Some."

"Every day? Once a week? Couple times a month?"

"Yeah."

"Which?"

"Month."

"Hmmm . . ."

The doctor washed his hands and started drying them with paper towels from a dispenser on the counter. Really, the doctor was almost invisible. The room, painted and scrubbed and lit by fluorescents, was so white that no other colors survived. Dr. Hess's white hair hid the upper half of his head, just as his long white smock hid most of his body. Everything was white. Every piece of furniture. Every apparatus. The only features that distinguished themselves against the background were the pink of the doctor's face and the pink of his hands, though the hands were now obscured by the white of the paper towels. Dr. Hess walked up and put a hand on his shoulder. Jonah started.

"Well then, let's have a look. Lift your shirt up, please."

Jonah looked down and watched the doctor's fingers poke into his tummy.

"This hurt?"

It didn't, at least not any more than it usually did when someone prodded your abdomen as hard as they could. Jonah winced and looked up to see the doctor noting the expression. The doctor pressed harder, forcing a lie out of his bowels, up his esophagus, and into the room. "Yeah. There."

"Hurts?"

"Yeah."

"Hmmm . . ."

Jonah wondered if he'd blown it. What if that wasn't the kind of spot that should hurt two to three times per month? He tried to read the doctor's face for clues, but he was expressionless, staring blindly off into the distance, searching Jonah's abdomen for the braille messages a disease might leave. "How about here?"

"I'm not sure."

"Now?"

"Ooh . . ."

"Hmmm . . ."

Again, Jonah searched the doctor's face to see if his lie was behaving consistently. The doctor must have seen the worry on Jonah's face because his bedside smile reappeared. His white teeth gleamed within the dark maw of a mouth which, joined with the white of the background, looked like the hole at the center of a big fleshy donut. It was such a disturbing vision that Jonah shook his head in an effort to dispel it.

"That hurt?" the doctor said as if surprised. But Jonah didn't see a way out.

"Um, yeah."

"Hmmm . . ." The hands went back to the chart and the donut followed them.

"Jonah, tell me, do you remember lifting anything heavy or straining yourself somehow, around the time the pains began?"

Jonah's eyes ached from the brightness. "Well, yeah, yeah, I did. In fact, I lifted an . . . anvil."

"An anvil?" The donut raised its eyebrows in disbelief.

"Yeah, a friend of mine has one." The eyebrows were still up. "In his basement. An anvil."

"Could you ask your mother to step in for a moment?"

*

They drove along in silence. Warm air blew in through the open windows of the car and Jonah enjoyed the sensation of the sun on his arm in much the same way a condemned man enjoys the sensations he encounters on the long walk to the room with the chair. He was feeling rather poetic.

Susan felt poetic too as she drove along, barely managing to keep her eyes on the road. Twice, she even had to slam on the brakes to keep from rear-ending someone. They stopped at a traffic light and Susan turned to Jonah, inhaling as if the exhale would bear the question, *"Jonah, isn't there something you'd like to tell me?"* but it didn't. She just let out a long, sad sigh. With her elbow on the wheel she looked out the window, chin resting on her palm. The light changed, but only Jonah noticed.

"Mom?"

"Hm?"

"Light."

"Oh."

She let the clutch out too quickly and they lurched fully into first gear. Both of their heads rocked in unison, then stopped as the car stalled. Susan looked at her son and smiled sheepishly, the glance so open and tender that it caught Jonah off guard. What the fuck was on her mind? Had there been some sort of stay of execution that no one had bothered to tell him about? Susan restarted the car and got them back on their way but reached over to rest her hand on Jonah's thigh and then proceeded to miss their exit. Jonah watched it as they passed, flabbergasted. This was the woman who stood around all afternoon on a football field so that she'd be better able to gauge how to signal exactly fifty feet before an intersection. He had never seen her miss an exit before in his life. When they took the next exit and stopped at the light, she reached up, touched the three razor parts he had shaved into the side of his head, and smiled lovingly even though she had made no secret of how much she hated that haircut. He watched her as she drove, a tough little woman working the cranks and levers of this huge piece of machinery, worn down and vulnerable in a world of corners and sharp objects. He leaned into her touch, feeling happy and accepted, suspicious, and more confused than ever.

*

Eventually, they pulled up in front of his school. It was late morning and the kids who had first lunch ran screaming back and forth, tearing up the blacktop like drunken savages. As nice as the ride had been, Jonah was loathe to be seen in the company of his mom and quickly started to open the door.

"Jonah? Wait a minute."

He slid down in his seat a little and put his back to the playground. "Yeah?"

"Am I a good mom?"

Not even ghosts had ever taken him aback as much as his mother's question. "Why, sure, you're the best mom in the whole world." He knew how that sounded, but he meant it and so made no amendments.

"I mean, if there were something that was really upsetting you, you'd tell me about it. Wouldn't you?"

"Mom. Of course." He meant that too. He meant it so much that it wasn't until his lunchtime, by himself at the corner of the playground that he realized he had lied.

*

Susan watched Jonah walk toward the school, expecting to see him greet a friend, talk to someone he knew, maybe even steal a few moments away from class because he thought she'd driven away, but none of that happened. Instead, Jonah hunched over, letting his head fall, drawing his shoulders in close, and walked toward the building as if he were bracing himself against the cold, ignoring the other children and the warm day, in a world of his own.

Susan pulled away from the school, steering and accelerating, scarcely seeing the road for the image of Jonah she held in her mind. His windbreaker, many sizes too big for him, hung from his body, and his haircut made him look ratty; he looked like a little homeless person. As the realization hit her she began to cry, so hard that she had to pull over. She parked and let the sobs overtake her.

*

The breeze that blew in through the open window to Jonah's bedroom coaxed a brief expression onto his face as he sat dozing at the foot of his bed. It returned moments later, more forcefully, and Jonah awoke.

"Hey, Dad." Jonah looked at his father, who, like all ghosts, flickered transparently in the warm spring air. He could see his father's gestures as he spoke, but the words broke into static, as if beyond broadcast range. Dan crossed the room, still speaking, and stood between Jonah and the window with a serious expression on his face. Jonah looked through his father at the wind in the trees and slipped back into sleep.

*

". . . in the end. Jonah? Can you hear me?"

Jonah opened his eyes. His father stood very close. He was practically invisible, but his words were clearly audible.

"I'm sorry, Dad. What did you say?"

Jonah felt his father sigh. "I was talking about the seasons."

"Ghosts are seasonal, aren't they? Angrier as it gets colder and nicer when it's warm?"

Dan shrugged. "Son, everything's seasonal. Didn't you hear any of what I said?"

"Sorry. You're barely there."

His father sighed again, the sound indistinguishable from the rushing wind. "Kid, do you know how I can tell the living from the dead?"

Jonah shook his head.

"The live ones are in a hurry. Even when they're sleeping, even when they're sitting there watching TV. Always hurrying." Dan paused. Jonah could hear the ice of his drink tinkling in its glass. He waited for his father's satisfied "*Ahhhh*," but it never came. "You're not in a hurry anymore, Jonah." The words faded beneath a wave of white noise, becoming ever more faint. "You're not dead, but you're not . . ."

Jonah lost consciousness. Asleep, he slumped slowly backwards. His mouth dropped open and he began to snore.

*

Jonah studied himself from above. The sound of labored breathing drifted heavily out of his open mouth as he hovered, free from thought. On the verge of drifting off toward a night's travel, he heard a knock at the door, and saw his body sit up in bed, still asleep. Jonah thought the words and watched himself speak.

"Umm, come in."

Susan opened the door and entered, standing tentatively in front of her son, unsure of what she should do with her arms. "Jonah, I need to talk to . . . oh my God, this place is a mess!"

Jonah looked around. She was right about that.

"How can you live like this? Oh my . . ." Her voiced trailed off in disgust. No longer unsure of herself, Susan rushed from atrocity to atrocity. ". . . this was a perfectly good . . . half-eaten . . . it's a good thing I . . . oh, for the . . ." she mumbled. Eventually, she wore herself out and plunked down on the bed beside Jonah. "Honey, this room is a sty."

"I know." Jonah had not intended for the thought to end there. His disembodied self began rolling out a long list of excuses, but the body remained mute, good only for a word or two.

Susan looked at the floor, not seeing the mess anymore, and inhaled slowly. "Jonah, I don't know how to say this so I'm just going to say it and get it out in the open and then we'll deal with it however. Okay?"

"Okay." He watched his mother hunch forward and look into his eyes.

"Okay. Dr. Hess says that what you've got might be a hernia and if the pains get worse or more frequent that would mean that's what it is and you'll need an operation. But he doesn't think that's what it is. He thinks it's an emotional thing and you're either making it up on purpose or it's psychosomatic and either way, you should talk to someone about it. To someone besides me. To a . . . man. Shrink. A man shrink."

"Okay."

"And your counselor at school, Mrs. . . . whatever, Mrs. Woods, she suggested it too. Do you even know her? Never mind. She thinks you should see one."

Jonah found he couldn't say anything.

"Jonah, I thought I could be both . . . I thought our lives were going to be perfect." Jonah watched as his body reached out, took his mother's hand, which lay forgotten at her side, and held it. She sighed and turned back around to take his hand with her other one. Her cheeks were wet with tears.

"Do you remember your dad?"

*

Jonah's memories of his father had coalesced into a single scene in his memory, a scene so stylized by endless repetition that it became like a creation myth—simple in form but bottomless in the depth of its images. In that scene, his father comes home from work, throwing the door open, and when Jonah runs to him, he is scooped up by the huge hands hanging from the ends of a suit, which lift him to the ceiling with a loud *"Atta boy,"* then stow him squarely on his father's hip, which Jonah rides to the liquor cabinet. His father makes a martini and asks Jonah questions about his day while Jonah burrows into the dark interiors of the suit coat and sends his answers up from amongst the smells of aftershave and tobacco, enjoying the rough crispness of his father's dress shirt and the cool silk of his tie. His father makes the drink with one hand and stirs it with his finger, which he gives to Jonah to lick.

"I remember him a little bit. He was tall, wasn't he?"

Susan wiped her tears with her wrists.

"And handsome. God, that man could make me laugh."

Jonah couldn't remember ever seeing his mom really crack up over something.

"He drank too much, you know."

"Yeah, you told me."

"I didn't really think about it until we had you, but when we did I started reading about it and realized . . . saw how much damage it could do. Honey, I was so scared that when he died, I figured we were saved. I figured I could do a better job than the both of us." She looked around the room.

"So here's the deal. You do what you want. You want to talk to someone, we'll do it, I'll help you, we'll find you someone you like. You don't want to, no one brings it up, nothing happens, we forget about it. And in the future, you bring it up, we do it. Okay?"

But Jonah could barely hear her. He'd floated down to the swing set in the backyard, unused for years, which Susan had somehow never gotten around to removing. The words his mother spoke swam through him like a school of fish, moving along without leaving a trace. His mother spoke again and the words hit his sleeping body in a series of soft splashes. He watched as they swam through him, away and downstream, into the night.

"Jonah, you're all I've got." She drew herself up and pulled him to her, but he couldn't feel her embrace.

*

Hi Ross.

Ross burped in his sleep and rolled over.

Don't be sad, Ross, look how good your life will be.

Ross Hand was about to move. Through a series of coincidences, his mother would stay out all night with a group of Jamaican businessmen, wake up next to one of them in the morning, and find she'd rediscovered love. In one year's time, after a courtship that involved fine dining and precious jewels, she'd marry and take her children to live in Jamaica. There, Ross would lose his baby fat, and between the Caribbean sun and the melanin that came from his Ghanian father, Ross would grow tall, brown, and confident. After receiving his MBA in the States, Ross would return to Jamaica to take a position in his stepfather's company, at whose helm he'd eventually sit. There was more, but Jonah had trouble seeing it.

He was suddenly feeling very much alone.

*

Jonah often wondered why he couldn't see his own future when he went dreaming. A full-length mirror hung on the door to Ross's closet, and Jonah floated over to it, looking for his reflection.

Nothing was there.

*

Jonah floated above his mom when he returned from the night's wanderings and watched her as she slept. She'd pulled herself up in a ball, but in spite of her efforts to hide it, Jonah could still see the lump growing within her breast like a set of rings. Inside each one, millions of smaller sets of rings shifted against one another, some linked, some mobile. Rings within rings within rings, expanding ever outward and inwardly more dense.

*

The only ghost Jonah saw the rest of that summer was on August 28. He looked up one day to see his dad making himself a drink at the liquor cabinet. When he poured the booze, he stirred it with his finger, but this time he licked it himself. Then he marched up to Jonah's room and promptly fell asleep.

*

KID SHIT

"JONAH. BEDTIME." Jonah turned and looked at Susan with a baleful expression. "C'mon, kid. You don't want to be tired for the first day of school do you?" she teased cheerfully.

Susan regretted the question immediately. Judging from the deep circles under Jonah's eyes, it was clinically impossible for him to be more tired. He looked her in the eyes for a long moment, then simply got up and headed for the stairs.

"You're not even going to put up a fight?"

Jonah kept walking. "Naah," he said.

Susan rose from her chair and rushed to the foot of the stairs as Jonah reached the top. "Jonah. Wait a minute."

He turned with agonizing slowness and looked down on his mother. She composed herself momentarily, as if hesitant. "Are you . . . are you on drugs?"

Jonah burst into laughter. "You think I'm . . ." he started, but fresh laughter overcame him and he had to steady himself against the banister, lost in open amusement. He wiped the moisture from the corners of his eyes. "No, Mom, I'm not on drugs." He turned his back on his mother, still laughing, and disappeared into his room.

*

Once the laughter subsided, Jonah found himself in a funk. Sitting on the edge of his bed, he produced a pack of matches from his pocket and began lighting them, slowly, one by one. He let each burn down until the pain in his fingertips became too great, then shook the match into lifelessness and threw it onto the pile of laundry at his feet. A half hour later, the smell of sulphur heavy in the air, he broke the final match out of the pack, lit it, and watched the red tip flare dramatically, then recompose itself into a tiny flame, clinging to the end. It grew gradually, consuming the match. When it had burned halfway down, Jonah tossed it into the laundry.

"That is the dumbest thing I ever saw."

"Shut up. You're not my dad." Jonah looked at Dan. The match passed its flame to the T-shirt it landed on. It began to spread.

"Put it out, son."

"No."

"Young man, are you testing me?"

Jonah looked at the ghost of his father defiantly. "Yeah. I'm testing you."

Dan straightened his tie and adjusted his coat. "Okay, have it your way." He tugged at his sleeves and took a sip from his drink but did not swallow, holding the fluid in his mouth while he inhaled deeply through his nose. When his lungs reached capacity, he expelled the mix of air and alcohol from his mouth in a sputtering column of flame. In an instant, the room was ablaze. The laundry roiled beneath a surging patina of liquid orange as the cloth fell into component parts. Posters blackened and curled away from the walls. The foot of the bed and most of the mattress roared as fire clung and then grew. A dry smell blistered Jonah's nostrils as oxygen vanished, and he leapt in pure panic, anticipating the moment when the fire from his burning clothes would feast on his skin. He bolted for the door, but Dan cut him off, so he veered away, crashing into the wall next to the closet and collapsing. He pulled himself up, shielding his eyes against the flames, and saw his father calmly purse his lips and puff, as if to blow out a candle. The room was instantly extinguished.

*

Jonah ran to the pile of clothes, rooting through the denim and cotton blends until he found the T-shirt where the match had landed. A single blackened hole the size of a quarter stood out on a field of brown cloth. Jonah scrunched the shirt and buried his face in it, relieved beyond belief. He looked up at Dan.

"Do I have your attention now? Because . . ."

"Jonah, what was that noise?" He could tell by the sound of his mother's voice that she had already reached the top of the steps. Before he could react, his father spoke in a perfect imitation of his son: "Sorry, Mom. I ran into the wall."

"Well, no more of that. I'm going to bed now, so keep it down."

Jonah responded in spite of himself. "Okay, Mom, goodnight."

He and Dan spoke in unison, but only one voice emerged from the two of them.

"Goodnight," Susan replied.

*

All summer long Jonah had looked forward to his father's return, saving up questions and rehearsing dialogue. Without their nightly chat he felt increasingly anchorless, and the wandering that had felt so soothing when it began now left him cranky and craving more upon his return in the morning. Relieved and happy to have his dad back, he found himself inexplicably sullen and withdrawn.

"Sorry about that," he said.

"Screw guilt," said his father, ever the lawyer.

"Then thanks."

"Better, much better." Dan climped atop the pile of laundry and looked around as if surveying his domain. "So," he said, addressing himself to Jonah, "what the fuck is your problem?"

"Well, it's just that you weren't here and I had so many questions and so much is happening and it's so weird and I'm scared . . ." Jonah's features became flat and red as he strained against the tears that flowed down his face.

"*Be-be-be-be-be-be-be,*" Dan mimicked in falsetto, pretending to wipe away tears.

"Why are you so mean to me?"

Dan materialized next to his son, suddenly contrite. Jonah felt an arm around his shoulders, a heavy warmth that he felt in his whole body. "Jonah, I'm dead. It's never going to be the way you want it to be. I'm not really here."

"Then I'm crazy."

"It's not that either, although that is one of the risks you're running. But there comes a point where words fail. The software up here," Dan tapped gently at Jonah's temple, "is smart enough to perceive the phenomenon, but not enough to process the explanation. You're actually quite advanced."

"Oh, great."

"Yeah, sucks, doesn't it?"

Jonah picked his nose and wiped it on his jeans. "I still can't know for sure if you really exist, can I?"

"No." Dan smiled, quite pleased with himself. "But whether I'm here or you're crazy, or neither, or both, you're involved in a dialectic."

"What does *that* mean?"

"It means that you must apply rigorous logic to our conclusions. Test 'em. Find out it they're right." Dan's smile glinted despite the darkness of the room. "Like with sawdust."

"Fat lot of good that did me."

"But you were on the right track, don't you see?"

Jonah changed the subject. "I'm in trouble, aren't I?"

"Yes, son, I'm afraid you are."

"What's going to happen?"

Dan searched for the words. "Has it ever occurred to you that I don't want to be here?"

"Then why don't you just leave me alone?"

"Whoa, now hold on. I'm happy to be here, really I am, but—this is words failing us again—*happy* doesn't really cover it. Don't you see, if left to my own devices, there are other things I'd go and do? Other things more appropriate to my nature?"

Jonah, suddenly exhausted, let his head rest in his hands and closed his eyes.

"Son, has it ever occurred to you that perhaps I'm here because you're holding me here?"

Jonah began snoring. Hesitantly, as if stealing, Dan ran his fingers through his son's hair, then disappeared.

*

How long had he been asleep? Jonah couldn't remember the last time he'd been awake. He floated above the waterfall trying to figure it out, but he couldn't.

"Jonah! Look out! Incoming!"

Ross splashed down next to him in the deeps below the falls and the impact knocked him out of his reverie. I'm not dreaming, he suddenly realized. I'm awake.

Coughing on the water he'd inhaled when Ross landed, Jonah thrashed frantically, gasping for air, then hauled himself to where the water was shallow enough to stand. He stood in the warm water, feeling the sand beneath his toes, panting and trying to figure out what the fuck had just happened.

*

Tommy, Bobby, and Ross hit the water in rapid succession and Jonah understood. It was Saturday and he and his friends had gone to the waterfall. He'd been the first off the cliff and the moment he'd lost contact with the earth, he'd slipped into dreaming, floating upward as his body fell. He didn't even remember hitting the water.

*

Sitting in class, Jonah looked at Ross, and they both looked up at the clock. Five minutes 'til lunchtime. Mr. Colson, their geometry teacher, drew on the blackboard, sputtering excitedly as he demonstrated.

"Don't you see? The asymptote approaches the axis, approaches the axis, closing the distance, closing the distance, but they'll never touch. Always approaching, never touching. Did I say never? Oh no, not never. The asymptote and the axis meet . . . in infinity!" Colson raised a finger and smiled with delight, great bushes of hair protruding from his ears. Jonah scribbled on a piece of paper and handed it across the aisle to Ross.

He means his head and his assymptote meet in infinity.

Ross read the note and responded.

Tote my p,ass (tote my ass).

Jonah struggled to compose a response. He was about to ink into creation a haiku that began with the five syllable line, "*If I could ass pee,*" when the bell rang.

*

Jonah and Ross banged their way into their lockers and retrieved their lunches. Walking down the hall, each began rooting through his bag.

"Whatcha get?" asked Ross.

"Um, looks like millet, beans, seaweed salad, and steamed vegetables."

Ross grimaced. "Man, how can you eat that shit?"

Jonah shrugged. "What'd you get?"

"The usual. Baloney on white, half a bag of Doritos, Skittles, M&M's, Ho-ho's . . ."

They passed through the big green doors and down the steps to the blacktop in back of the school. The building formed a great "U" and a long chain-link fence topped with curling rows of barbed wire closed them off from the athletic fields and the street below. Like stars in their own little prison film, Jonah and Ross walked the yard, nodding in recognition of this clique or that as they made their way to their part of the playground, the northwest corner, where the red brick ended and the fence began and weed trees had been allowed to establish a thicket in the broken surface.

Jonah stopped. "Who's that?" he asked, pointing to the two boys talking with Sara and Kim.

"Steve Schrank," Ross answered. "He started hanging out this summer. Cool shoes, huh?" Jonah realized immediately that the other kid was dead. The ghost hovered next to Kim barefoot, briskly rubbing his small hard-on and fingering the noose that pinched the skin of his neck.

"Well, I've never seen him before," said Jonah.

"That's because you *stopped* hanging out this summer."

"I hung out . . . with you . . ."

"Not exactly, Jonah. I hung out with you." They drew close to the gang. "And you *have* seen Steve before. He was with us each time I dragged you out to the mall. You just never spoke to him."

Jonah said nothing. He racked his brain, searching for memories from the summer, but none came. He felt sick.

"Hey Jonah, hey Ross," Steve said.

"Hi, Steve," said Ross.

"HI JONAH! HI JONAH! HI JONAH!" cried the masturbater.

Jonah looked at the ground wishing he were asleep. He wished it so hard, it came true.

*

In the dream he stood on the playground, watching his friends laugh and talk. The breeze held the first hints of autumn dryness and rushed past him, blue like the sky. The bell rang and he watched as his body turned from the spot where they stood and walked reluctantly toward the building along with his friends. Look at me, he thought, I'm just like them. Sandra jabbered glibly, simultaneously offended and amused by the gossip she was dealing. Sara walked confidently, popular now, knowing guys were checking her out, and not minding. Kim, poor Kim, slumping and grasping *Crime and Punishment* to her meager chest. Bobby Brockman led the pack—athletic, handsome, conceited. Steve followed like a lieutenant. And bringing up the rear, Jonah and Ross, the big dumb guy and the little smart one. Jonah watched himself as he sleepwalked away from the group. Ross went and gathered him, guiding him into the building calmly, like it happened all the time. Jonah loved them. They were so beautiful. He could see their hearts beating. He could see their glands secreting hormones. He watched them disappear into the building and then looked up at the sky.

*

There was no way of telling how long his dreaming self spent standing there on the playground. Vaguely aware of his physical self somewhere inside the building—he could feel himself moving in behind a desk and sitting down—the sensation was peripheral. A tiny voice inside him wondered where the waters of sleep had gone, but the voice had to shout to be heard and soon grew tired. Looking at the sky, he noted the ice crystals of the cirrus clouds far above and wondered how high he could get. He considered trying, but floated over into the dumpster and inspected the corrugated fibers of a cardboard box instead.

*

Within a week Jonah could access dream time at will. Imagine how handy. Angry at your friends? When you view them through these easy-to-use dream lenses, you'll be charmed into forgetfulness by their biological perfection and spiritual interrelatedness. Dull lecture? Simply ease the seat back and drift away on successive waves of secondary reality. Not only will you not suffer the grinding boredom of your classes, but you'll return to find that your body has taken notes and answered questions too! At night you can set yourself up doing homework, then float down and watch TV with your mom. As for ghosts, why all you have to do is close your eyes and watch them disappear.

*

Don bit Susan's neck and she moaned, stretching away to give him more room to work. He pressed in and she gasped. Naked, she wrapped her legs around him and gripped him to her. Don changed his angle and entered.

"Wait a minute . . . Don . . . what are you doing?"

Don looked back at her through heavily lidded eyes, moustache all over the place. "Making love?"

"Not without a condom, you're not."

"Would it be so bad if we had a baby?" Don whined, collapsing against her.

In a few moments Don fetched a condom and their lovemaking resumed, but Susan found herself hurrying.

*

The sunrise crested and Susan sprang out of bed like she always did, ready to arm wrestle with whatever the new day might offer. She went to the window and opened it wider, letting in more fresh air and looking at the sun in the treetops while her skin tingled with the cool air of a summer's morning. She enjoyed a few moments of empty-headedness, stretching where she stood. Fully awake, she went to the gym mat at the foot of her bed and began her morning yoga.

Her first posture was Denial About Her Son's Antisocial Behavior, a well-practiced position that had her tending to the details of what was wrong without actually acknowledging them to herself. She held the position, breathing deeply. From there, she stretched into Ignoring Being Upset. Susan wasn't even sure she could have a baby these days, but the fact that Don even said the words upset her—she liked things the way they were. Calm and centered within that position, she moved to the next, False Optimism, and its corollary posture, Bravado, progressing confidently through her routine, a short one compared to the longer one she did evenings after work. When she finished she rose, threw her nightie in the hamper, and headed for the shower.

*

The bathroom included a massive skylight, which Susan had built so she could keep plants that thrived in a warm, moist environment. Gray daylight illuminated the opening and steam rose from the cast-iron tub, ringed with a simple white liner, where Susan showered. She held her head back, rinsing away shampoo, while the water drummed against her skull. Reaching behind her in unconscious motion, she tightened the cold water tap slightly, increasing the heat of the mix.

Suds cascaded down her body. She ran her hands along her limbs, pushing the shampoo from her, feeling its slickness on her skin. She rested her hands on her belly, soft and round, then inhaled and crossed her arms over her chest. She placed her hands on the outside of each breast and found the lump.

*

Susan finished her oatmeal and looked through the kitchen door to the "Women's Health" section of her library. She'd made breakfast in a slow, distracted panic, waiting for Jonah to leave so she could find out what she should do. Her fingers strayed involutarily to the lump.

"Are you ready for your quiz?" she asked.

Jonah looked back at her through deeply lidded eyes.

"Um, probably."

"Jonah. You either know the first twenty elements or you don't."

"I do. Sort of."

"And they are . . ."

"Um, well, hydrogen, helium. Librium. Um . . ."

"Oh, Lord. Go do the dishes."

*

When he was done cleaning, Jonah poked his head out of the kitchen and spoke.

"Have a good day, Mom. Mom?"

Susan spoke without looking up from the book she held. "You too, dear . . . Jonah, did you put the brush back in its rack?"

Jonah looked and saw that he hadn't.

"Yeah."

"Okay, see you. And regardless of how you do on the quiz, you and I are going to have a little quiz of our own tonight."

"Okay. Mom?"

"Yes, honey?"

"Is something wrong?"

"No dear, why? Why would something be wrong?"

"Because you're standing on one foot."

"Oh." Susan instantly dropped down to two and, for the first time in her life, blushed in front of her son.

*

As soon as Jonah left for school, Susan sat down next to the phone in the front hallway and called her doctor, fingers trembling as she dialed. It's nothing, she told herself. Caught early and probably benign. But her throat felt itchy and her temples throbbed.

"Dr. Mengele's office."

"Hello, Vivian, this is Susan Hart. I've found a lump on my breast and I'd like to make an appointment to come in and have it looked at."

"Of course, Susan, I'll just . . . I'm sorry, can you hold a minute?"

Soft jazz came over the line.

*

She felt the lump through the fabric of her blouse, exploring it with vague dread and staring at the floor. Specks of dust, illuminated by the rays of sunlight in the hallway, floated tranquilly, neither rising nor falling, wandering according to tiny indoor currents. Suddenly the front door, left closed but not latched by Jonah, yielded to the pressure of a summer breeze and blew open. It hit the radiator with a crash and wind was everywhere, rushing into the living room, up the stairs, and over Susan. The pages of the notebook flapped unnoticed on her lap while Susan looked up. A warm smell washed her face and filled her nostrils, obliterating the music in the handset as sound retreated and Susan watched the world go dark. Scenes from *The Movie That Was Her Life* began to flash before her eyes.

*

As her first fiancé Greg Witherspoon bore down into her, Susan gasped with a sudden rush of pleasure. She came, arching her back and crying out as Greg splashed inside her, the muscles along his spine rising, locked, until he collapsed onto her breast. The tall, dry stalks of the hayfield rustled in the nighttime breeze. Greg suckled, eyes closed. Susan stared at the stars.

"Don't ever leave me, okay?" she said.

"What?"

She craned her neck to look Greg in the eye. "Don't ever leave me."

"Susan. We're engaged."

"I know . . ." she cooed happily, pulling Greg close for a kiss. "But I'm not going to see you all summer."

"I know . . ." Greg joined her in happy longing. "But fall is soon. And we'll be sophomores." He lay on his back alongside her and looked up. "I promise," he said.

"Promise what?"

"To never leave you."

She pulled him close again then relaxed, drawing figures on his stomach with all five fingers of her right hand.

*

There they went, the index and the middle. The table saw grabbed them and they were gone, lost in the sawdust beneath the machine. Susan's head snapped back, damaging two of the vertebrae in her neck, then lurching forward, she cracked her ribs against the table's edge. A fine red mist floated momentarily above the roaring blade and she managed two steps before collapsing on the floor. Fellow students rushed to her side.

"Susan, are you okay?" one of them asked.

"Oh my God, look at her hand."

"Someone . . ." Susan started, but couldn't continue.

"Someone call an ambulance!"

"There's no time—I'll drive her."

"Someone please get my fingers. Please get . . ." she whispered, but nobody heard.

*

Susan, seated in the chair in her hallway, watched in shock as Greg Witherspoon lost control of his Corvair and flew out of the convertible as it landed in the ditch. His neck broke as he flipped over the windshield and his body turned somersaults until he wedged himself between a brace of saplings. Susan's rush of tears at the sight gave way to disbelief; how could I be seeing this? No one was there. Greg's elongated neck twisted to reveal glassy eyeballs, knees gathered beneath him as if he'd fallen asleep praying. Susan shuddered; the motion dispelled the image. Instead, she saw herself sitting in the front pew at Greg's funeral in her neck brace, blue suit, and matching hat, mangled hand wrapped in gauze and resting on her lap.

"Are you sure you wouldn't rather go home?" Greg's mom asked.

Susan winced as she turned to respond. "No. I'm fine. Thanks."

The two women looked at each other across a sea of loathing. Flanked by all of Greg's relatives and everyone he'd ever known, she struggled against the pain, watching Mrs. Witherspoon's skin hang from her face in great sagging folds. "I really think you should go lie down." She frowned.

*

"Mrs. Hart?" The receptionist was back on the line.

"Yes?" Susan heard her own voice say.

"How's tomorrow at 10:30?"

"That would be fine," said her voice.

*

Tammy Fayette shaped the cherry of the Kool they'd stolen from her mom's purse against the silvered top of the picnic table. "Dew yew know what ah'm sayin'?" she asked, incredulously. She and Tammy, dressed in identical halter tops and blue jeans, sat behind the PX at Ft. Benning, drinking coffee from a thermos and killing time.

"What if I don't do it right?"

"Honey, don't you worry. Just put that thing in your mouth and you'll see. It's the shortest leash in the world."

*

Susan laughed out loud at the thought and wondered where Tammy Fayette had ended up. Now that she thought of it, Tammy was one of the few real friends she'd ever had.

*

Tammy talked, but something was different. The angle of the sun maybe.

"I know you think that. I can even see *how* you think that. But it's not true, Susie, she needs you right now. She won't ask for anything, that's not her way, but that don't mean she doesn't need it. Do you see what I'm sayin'?" Tammy reached out and touched Susan's forearm. Susan pulled it away as she began her sentence.

"Do you know what she did when the telegram came? Nothing! Nothing. Her husband's dead, his plane's shot down, and she just went inside, went on with her day."

Tammy reached out again, placing her hand on the spot where Susan's arm had been, and the two friends sat, not speaking.

*

"Dan, you're going too fast, you're going to get a ticket."

Dan smiled and guided the Porsche around the bend. Susan, in her shades and scarf, held on for dear life. Trees crowded the tiny road. Coming out of the curve, they banked in the opposite direction, passenger and driver leaning into the turn.

"Dan, I mean it."

Dan continued smiling and kept his eyes on the road.

A sign approached and then disappeared, *"Lake Placid, 129 miles."* Susan tightened the knot in the scarf that held her hairdo in place and gripped the armrest on the door as the tiny sports car held the road. Dan looked at her, then leaned right into the next turn. Susan let herself get carried left.

"Dan, why are you doing this?"

Dan abruptly pulled over and they came screeching to a halt, tilting dangerously toward the ditch. He turned to Susan, smiling tightly, dried spittle collected at the corners of his mouth. He hovered above her on the uphill side of the car.

"What, Susan, why am I doing *what?*"

Susan leaned back into her door. "Um. Driving. Too fast. Driving too fast." Her eyes rested on his thighs.

"I. Am. Not. Driving. Too. Fast." Dan pounded the dash rhythmically, teeth clenched against the force of the words. Susan could feel the force of the blows in the door behind her. She raised her eyes to meet his, then lowered them to Dan's hands where they gripped the wheel. The car's powerful engine idled, as the two sat in silence. After five minutes, Dan got out and pulled the *"Just Married"* signs off the hood and the rear bumper, flinging them into the ditch. Returning to his seat, he put the car back into gear and pulled away.

*

Susan filled the silver kettle from the tap and turned the knob for the right back burner. The starter clicked four times in rapid succession, then erupted into flame. It was 4 a.m. by the clock above the doorway. When the water boiled, she made a cup of tea and brought it to the breakfast table, where she sat down.

When she awoke, the clock read 5 a.m., dim sunlight was preceding the dawn, and Dan had caught his coat on the doorknob as he entered the house. His attempts to disentangle himself failed and he fell to the floor heavily. Susan rose slowly, pouring her cold tea into the sink, setting the flame beneath the kettle again, and listening to Dan stumble up the stairs. When she heard the floorboards creaking in their bedroom she moved to shut the front door and saw, in the stillness of the dew-covered morning, Dan's Mercedes parked on top of their tulips. She closed her eyes, leaned into the jamb, and listened to the birds singing in the new morning.

*

Susan watched from the hallway as she went to answer the phone—the call from the State Trooper—but the scene became confused. She saw herself at their house in the Philippines when she was a girl and remembered that the phone wasn't ringing at all, she was dreaming. She went downstairs to answer it and found her father in the kitchen. How old was she, six, seven? It made no sense to her at the time, but now she could understand what she saw. Her father's eyes had that faraway viscous shine indicating that he was very, very drunk, and, because he was stripped to the waist, Susan could see the process of his aging where the skin on his frontside had fallen, stretching across his collarbones and gathering thickly at the waist. He'd left the screen door open and moths bashed into the overhead light. Colonel Jonah McCoy looked down thoughtfully as he brought his clenched fist and forearm as close as he could stand it to the front burner of the stove and then moved his arm slowly lengthwise along the flame. She watched quietly while he did first one arm and then the other, the smell of singed hair filling her nostrils, thinking, what are you doing, Daddy, but not daring to say it because sometimes, when you interrupted, Daddy yelled.

*

She walked away quietly, into the darkness of the rest of the house, but now it was *her* house and Jonah, fifteen, lay asleep in his bed. He'd kicked off the covers, exposing himself completely, oh God, my baby, he's cracking up, how can I save him if I can't give him my strength? These days, when Susan would watch his sleeping body, it was as if his soul were gone. She looked at her son and thought, he's dead. I can't save him because he's already dead.

*

"Jonah?"
"Sorry, Mom. What'd you say?"

Although Jonah could see that he was at the dinner table, he had no idea how he'd gotten there.

"I said . . ." Susan repeated her story and Jonah attempted to regain his bearings. ". . . I mean, can you believe it? Right there in the check-out line?"

"No, Mom."

"You'd never do a thing like that. Would you?"

"No, Mom, I . . ." Jonah began coughing uncontrollably.

"I know. Too much cayenne."

He recoiled, salivating profusely, having just noticed the searing pain in his mouth.

"Mom, oh my God," he managed to say. "What's in this?"

"I don't know. Squash?"

"Well, it tastes terrible."

Susan, who already had her elbows on the table, put her head in her hands and abruptly began to weep.

"Um, well, it's not so bad. I mean . . ." Jonah stared at his mother in raw disbelief. "Mom?"

He went to her and put his arm around her, unsure if it was the right thing to do.

"Mom, are you okay?"

"Oh, Jonah, I have cancer."

*

From his sudden vantage point in the far corner, where the cabinets met the ceiling, he could see himself comforting his mother and his mother gradually calming down. Time ceased flowing and Jonah floated, not noticing whether it took seconds or hours. He drew gradually closer, honing in on her bosom, trying to remember what it was like to suckle. The words his waking self spoke to his mother were muffled, and when he opened his eyes, he could see the hole the biopsy had left in her breast and how the countless millions of plastic six-pack rings were spreading from it like ants out of a hill toward the rest of her body.

*

Jonah stood before his mother. "Cancer?"

"I'm afraid so."

He thought about it. "Are you going to die?"

"Jonah! What kind of question is that?"

"Well, I don't know. I mean, what did the doctor say?"

"She said we do the mastectomy, then a round of chemotherapy, and then we see."

"So you're not going to die."

"Jonah! She said we'll see."

"But she didn't say, 'You're gonna die.'"

"No, but . . ."

"Well, that's what I wanted to know!"

Susan tsked and threw a series of sidelong glances. Jonah went back to his chair. After a while, he put another forkful of ratatouille in his mouth, knowing full well what it tasted like and eating it anyway.

"Are you gonna go bald?"

"Jonah!"

*

THE GRAPEST EYE

SEATED AT THE FOOT OF HIS BED, Jonah hovered at the edge of sleep. The random wash of thought slowed 'til each image became a photograph in his mind's eye, a single point of contemplation. He could see his mother's fierce blue eyes red from crying, when his father lit a cigarette and dispelled the image.

"Morning," he said, cupping his hand around the flame.

"Hi, Dad."

Dan exhaled happily, great plumes of smoke coming out each nostril. "Nothing like the first smoke of the day!"

"Where do you buy those things, anyway?"

"I don't 'buy' anything," he said, clicking the Zippo closed and returning it to his pocket. "Though what I wouldn't give for a little change in my pocket . . ."

He turned with a sweeping gesture and said, "Jonah, I'm not here," then caught himself. "But you can see me," he mused, "so that makes me . . ." He put a finger to his lips, pensive. "Words! Words are the problem! Worthless things." He gathered himself. "Jonah, if I could spend money, I'd be real. But you can see me, so I am. D'you see?"

"Mom's got cancer." As soon as he said it, Jonah suddenly noticed his father sitting right next to him.

"I know, kid." His voice was close, reassuring.

"Is she gonna be okay?"

"I can't see the future, you know that."

Jonah started crying. "What am I going to do?" he moaned, leaning into his father. Dan disappeared instantly.

"How can I express this?" he continued, materializing astride the windowsill. "Let me try this. Watch."

"Watch what?"

Dan looked at Jonah impishly and turned his head to indicate the window.

"What?"

Dan repeated the gesture.

"So?"

Dan tilted his head again, gesturing toward the window. Jonah rolled off the bed and went over to take a look. "I don't see what . . . whoa! Are those fish?"

Jonah pressed his hands against the windowpanes, then recoiled. "They're cold," he said, looking over at his dad. "Are we . . . We're underwater!"

Dan smiled, then raised his eyebrows and, looking Jonah in the eye, held out his raised index finger.

"What?" said Jonah.

Dan smashed his fist through one of the panes. Cold black water surged in, destroying the window in an instant and lifting Jonah to the ceiling.

"Aaaaaaaaaaaaa . . ." The water closed around his head, snatching the cry from his throat and extinguishing it with a short gurgling sound. He thrashed wildly, completely underwater.

Several thoughts competed for Jonah's attention, all equally compelling.

"The window!" one said.

"Don't be stupid!" said another.

"This, this can't be happening," a third stammered.

"Dad!"

In spite of himself, the cry burst from Jonah's burning lungs and he was forced to inhale. Only instead of water, he brought in air and felt himself drop. He hit the ground with a thud, looked up, and saw his father.

"See, son, you can't breathe underwater until you absolutely have to."

Jonah fainted. When he came to a few minutes later, his head was in his father's lap and Dan was stroking his hair soothingly. "You're going to have to take a stand, kid. You're going to have to decide what to turn your back on and what to face. Eventually, you're just going to have to take a stand."

*

Floating near the ceiling, Jonah watched his mother watch him sleep. She's broken her own rule, he thought. She promised me she'd never invade my space. Susan stood three feet back from the foot of Jonah's bed, hovering in the middle of the room as surely as Jonah hovered near the ceiling, hands crammed into the pockets of her jeans. At first Jonah thought she was standing on her toes but when he looked closer, he saw it wasn't so. She was just standing there staring.

When she left the room, he followed her, watching her crawl back into her dark bed and curl up in a ball. He thought about her womb and in an instant, was there—but not there—this was the stomach. The digestive acids were all around him and he didn't mind, one place was like any other, but when he thought about the womb a second time, nothing happened. Instead, he and that night's supper moved along into the small intestine where they waited in line for their turn to become shit. Jonah tried to opt out but wasn't successful until his third attempt. Back in the room, he tried to turn and look at his mother, to see if her cancer was spreading, but the currents were stronger than he was and bore him away before he had a chance.

*

It's amazing how from high, high above the world, cars look just like little ants. Those *are* ants, Jonah realized, hovering a half inch off the ground. The ant hole pulled at him and Jonah, powerless to resist, felt himself carried through the tunnels, watching the ants work while they sang company songs. It's a little-known fact that ants don't need sleep. Instead of using the extra waking hours for recreation, they use them to get more work done. Jonah listened to their song. *"We are ants . . . we are ants . . . we are ants . . ."*

*

Jonah's momentum carried him along through the wall and into the earth, angled slightly downward, into the organic matter contained within the topsoil. The soil here was rich. Years ago Susan decided that they would replace their grass with ground cover and stopped raking the leaves and watching bacteria convert ammonia into nitrogen, he could see the efficacy of his mother's decision. Mr. Erlichmann was fond of saying that you can't get something for nothing, but all Jonah had to do was to look around at all the rich topsoil to see that that was bullshit.

He was moving fast, from one yard to another and progressively lower and lower. Looking up through the dirt he could see houses, and further up, the stars. Am I slowing down? He thought he might be, but it was hard to tell. He remembered that there was a graveyard at the very end of his street and, figuring that it would be a kick, he set his heart parallel to the houses and adjusted his trajectory, but neither of those things happened. He continued downward through the subsoil and into the first of the three aquifers that lay beneath his neighborhood. Things were simpler there. There was less to look at.

*

Jonah had gone miles and miles and had slowed considerably. At one point he tried to pull out of his descent, but he hadn't been able to and was now convinced he was incapable of independent movement. He was gradually slowing and, he assumed, would soon stop. But what would happen then? How long would it take for the batteries of his consciousness to run out? Back in the world, they'd think he'd slipped into a coma and would use machines to keep him alive. But eventually, his body would die. And what then? Would he be there forever? He didn't mind. One thing was very much like another. One thing was exactly like another. This had to have happened before; he couldn't be the only one. How many other bubbles of disembodied consciousness were trapped beneath the earth's crust? It didn't matter. Or did it? He couldn't tell.

*

Jonah found he'd stopped moving.

. . . stopped moving.

Susan wasn't able to sleep, so she went back in to watch her son, who slept so soundly she was able to pull up a chair without waking him. His window was open, but the atmosphere of his room remained undisturbed, filling Susan's thoughts with the smell of his dirty clothes, and with something vaguely sweet. She studied his face; he was like a dead thing.

Gathering the loose folds of her nightgown about her knees, she found herself remembering the nighttime feedings in this very room, realizing what she really wanted to do was nurse him. She smiled, but then remembered her upcoming mastectomy and sank into despair.

Jonah's body jerked.

*

With a violent motion, a wave shot through his spine, sending his feet and his head in opposite directions and blowing the blankets right off him. Susan could see the muscles along his abdomen rising like dots when he exhaled. His lungs pumped air into his trachea, but his larynx was locked and all that came out was, *"Nng! Nng!"*

"Jonah!"

Susan ran to her son, but the force of his movements knocked her back. Looking up from the floor, she saw the muscles along his spine and in his legs tensing in a frenzy that sent the small of his back two feet up off the mattress.

. . . his body would die. And what then? Would he be there forever? He didn't mind. One thing was very much like another. One thing was exactly like another. This had to have happened before; he couldn't be the only . . .

. . . his body would die. And what then? Would he be there forever? He didn't mind. One thing was very much like another. One thing was exactly like another. This had to have happened before; he couldn't be the only . . .

Jonah hit the mattress, lay still for thirty seconds, flopped again, then went flaccid. Susan knew that if she just sat there, her son was going to die. She forced herself up, placed one hand on his forehead as if to brush the hair away, the other on his thigh, and felt Jonah give one last shudder beneath her.

Oh, thought Jonah, I haven't stopped.

*

Susan's touch nudged Jonah into a vein of groundwater, sandwiched between granite slabs, miles beneath the earth's surface. Its current was slow, only inches per week, but it reconnected him to the life ebbing from his body back in the room. When Susan's hand touched his forehead, a part of him began to flow out of the aquifer, connected somehow by the combination of his mother's touch and contact with the water table. The rest of him remained stuck, however, outside the vein. Jonah emerged from stasis to the realization that he couldn't stretch that far—that before his belly made it all the way back to his mom, the fibers of his consciousness would dissipate and he would cease to be. But when Susan touched him with her second hand, the rest of him was drawn along too. He accelerated through the widening fissures in the rock, noticing salinity and suddenly shooting straight out into the Chesapeake Bay. The sun warmed him as he spread thin upon the waters, but the estuary where Jonah had spent his first nine months gathered him back up and pulled him into the Potomac River. He hit the treatment plant, slammed his way through the maze of pipes hidden beneath his city, and flowed into the plumbing of his own house, shooting out of the toilet in a blue arc so intense it left tiny wisps of smoke in the air as he reentered his body. He was moving so fast that when he opened his eyes and saw his mom, he almost blew right through the front of his own face.

*

He found himself sitting on his bed with his mother, hair damp and slightly out of breath, listening to the sounds of the birds through the open windows. Jonah realized that he was completely naked and grabbed the sheet to cover his midsection. That made Susan laugh.

"Christ, Jonah, it's not as if . . . whoo, what's that smell?"

"Oh my God. Look."

Jonah presented his arms and legs for his mother to see. All the hair had been singed off.

*

At the breakfast table, neither one said a word. Jonah ate his oatmeal and sipped alfalfa tea as if nothing had happened. Susan, on the other hand, seemed to have developed a facial tic. She pushed her food around in her bowl and looked from side to side, on the verge of a question that continually failed to materialize. Instead of speaking, she'd poke her food and exhale sharply through her nose.

When Jonah finished his breakfast, he took both their bowls over to the sink and washed them, then kissed his mom on the forehead and went to get ready for school.

"See you, Mom."

"See you!" To say that her voice was "high-pitched" would be a gross understatement.

*

After her son left, Susan went to work. What else was there to do? Amazingly, she found herself going about her business, talking to people, making decisions, all with an inner detachment that made her feel powerful. What struck her most as she went through her day was the look she saw in her son's eyes as he kissed her on the forehead and said goodbye. Jonah was different. It wasn't just that he was obviously no longer a child, though that did begin to explain it. There was a toughness to him now. It dawned on Susan that her son was in the middle of a crisis that he'd been dealing with for a long, long time, though how she'd missed it until now was beyond her.

*

She took lunch at her desk, nibbling carrot sticks. It was obvious to her that she was going to have to talk to Jonah about it, but when and to what end were not immediately apparent. She was chewing, in deep thought, when Don stuck his head in the door.

"Susan, can we talk?"

"Don, now isn't . . ."

But he was already in.

*

Don shut the door behind him. "Susan, we've got to talk. I can't take it anymore."

Susan looked at him across her desk. He looked like he was about to be sick.

"Susan, I love you!"

"Oh Don, Jesus Christ . . ."

"I mean it. I really do. I want to get . . ."

"Don't say it. I mean it, Don . . ."

"But I do, I want to m . . ."

"Don . . ."

". . . marry you, Susan, I want to marry you!"

"Get out, Don . . ." Susan grabbed him by the arm and led him from her office.

"But I . . . but you . . ."

"Out!"

They faced each other across the open doorway.

"But, baby—"

Susan couldn't hear the rest. She'd shut the door.

*

THE OLD MAN AND THE SEA

ROSS AND JONAH ENJOYED THE WALK TO SCHOOL, partially because anything was better than school, but also because the alleyways, easements, and rights-of-way they took represented a way of life rapidly disappearing as the recurrent seasons carried them inexorably into adulthood. The adult world has its own way of viewing things and, though they didn't speak of it, Jonah and Ross both felt newly conscious as they walked along the top of the low brick wall that took them between two houses. This used to be their secret way and now, balancing lazily with a hand against one of the bay windows they passed, Jonah realized his presence might seem threatening in a way it hadn't been when he was little. They fell silent until they reached the alley.

"Shit!"

"Dude, what's your problem?"

"I didn't do my book report," Jonah said.

"Shit," agreed Ross.

"You do yours?"

"Yeah."

"We were supposed to read *The Old Man and the Sea*, right?"

"*The Old Man in the Pee!*"

Ross drew Hemingway's novella out of his back pocket and held it aloft like an Olympic torch as he ran in pantomime slow-motion.

"I'm open! I'm open!" Jonah screamed, sprinting up the alley and turning a buttonhook. Ross hit him with the book at three paces and Jonah, tucking in the reception, set his stiff arm out against the world in general.

"Was it good?"

"Good? Look at it. Hundred-fifty pages, max. And look at the size of the print!"

Jonah watched Ross shifting about uncomfortably while he fished around in the pocket of his windbreaker, finally coming up with a small sheaf of papers, battered and folded down to pocket-size, which he began to run with.

"What's that?"

"Pure fucking genius, that's what."

Jonah gave Ross a look.

"Dude, it's the book report."

"You dork! Mitchell said you had to type it, and also if anyone brought him pages that were folded or stained, they'd lose a letter grade!"

"Oh." Ross looked down at his report, deflated.

"Jesus, Ross, you are so dumb."

Silence fell as the two boys cut between a garage and a fence, overrun with vines.

"Jonah, I want you to stop being mean to me."

"What are you talking about—I'm never mean to you."

"Yes, you are. You didn't used to be. But now you are."

"Like when?"

"Like just now. I'm not stupid. And I can't help it that I'm fat."

Jonah almost said, *"Oh, Ross, you're not fat,"* then realized that he couldn't really say that.

"Ross, I'm sorry. I didn't mean it."

"I know. But it really hurts my feelings."

"I'm sorry."

"It's okay. Is it 'cause of your mom?"

"Nah."

Jonah looked up, squinting in the quickening wind, and saw that the sky had become completely gray and overcast. The boys began to hurry.

*

They cut through a series of hedgerows and made their way into the clearing next to the football field as the first drops of rain began to fall. The other students, approaching the building from more usual angles, were hurrying to make it before the rain began to fall in earnest.

"You know, Jonah, you can tell me stuff."

For a moment, Jonah considered telling Ross the whole thing: his dad, the ghosts, his dream travels, everything. "No," he said instead. "I'm okay."

*

The storm front reached Jonah and Ross halfway across the football field. By the time they arrived at the main doorway, they were soaked right down to their underwear.

*

Mr. Mitchell looked up at the class. "Pass your papers forward, please."

The class began going through the motions of retrieving and handing in their book reports. Jonah stared out the window.

More than anything else, he was pissed—he had more important things to worry about than some old dude who couldn't handle the sea anymore. Also, the pressure of rain-soaked underwear against his skin was making his butt itch and sent him rolling from one flank to the other in an attempt to scratch it without actually reaching into his trousers. He drummed the desktop with his fingertips and looked out the window at the thunderheads.

"Is that everyone? Jonah?"

"Huh?"

Jonah had absolutely no idea what had been said.

"Do you have anything for me?"

Jonah looked to Ross, but he was just grinning along with the rest of the class who thought Jonah was clowning for their benefit.

"Your book report, Jonah. You did do your book report, didn't you?"

"Um, no. Sir. I, uh, didn't."

"That's nothing to be proud of, Jonah."

The class brightened at what they took to be the punch line, but Jonah ground his teeth, barely able to control his temper. So you know what's on my mind, huh? Then maybe you could tell me why there's no hair on my forearms. Or, while you're at it, perhaps you could tell me a little about the dead kid who's standing on your desk. Dick. Can't even grow a real mustache, telling me I'm proud . . .

"Jonah?"

"What?!"

The class gasped audibly.

"Take that tone again with me, young man, and you'll find

yourself in the principal's office, lickety-split."

Ross beamed, hoping everyone knew Jonah was his best friend.

"Hand, what is this?"

All attention was suddenly on Ross.

"My book report?"

"Is that what you'd call it? A book report?"

"Umm, well . . ."

*

Lickety-split. Jonah rolled the words around in his mouth, muttering to himself. Son of a bitch. Threatening me, and he's such a geek he thinks lickety-split still means something. Asks me a rhetorical question and then tells me I'm proud. Threatening me. Can't even grow a decent mustache. Fuckface.

The sky was dark and electric, and since no daylight was coming in to disperse it, the fluorescent light filled the room with a nighttime quality that burdened Jonah as much as his anger. Dozens of ghosts were staring in through the windows of the first floor classroom, and Jonah noticed at least half as many standing right in the room, watching the proceedings. Dead kids, mostly. Just watching.

*

". . . class, and what we have here is a perfect example of what not to do . . ."

Mitchell held Ross's paper up for the class to see. Ross's lower lip began to tremble, and Jonah could see that if Mitchell continued to make an example of him, Ross was going to cry.

"Leave him alone."

Mitchell, amazed, stopped in mid-sentence.

"I'm sorry, what did you say?"

Jonah sighed, wondering where he should begin. "You heard me. Stop being such a dick."

"Well, young man, you just bought yourself a suspension."

"Fine. You gonna write me a hall pass or walk me down?"

"Oh, I'll write you your hall pass. But first, I want to say something that I think will be of benefit to everyone."

Jonah almost took issue with that, but let it go.

"It seems that some of you don't know this, so I suppose I'm going to have to tell you, that the ninth grade, technically, is your freshman year of high school. And high school is important because it's one of the points of transition between childhood and adulthood. Now, some of you seem to have grasped this and, accordingly, we treat you with the respect that young adults deserve. But those of you who insist on behaving childishly will find the going very rough. Very rough, indeed. Citizenship has many, many privileges, but it also has its responsibilities, and if you choose to ignore them, you'll find yourself excluded from many of the things that the rest of us take for granted. Now Jonah, you're going home for two days. And I honestly hope you'll reflect on what's been said here. And, so you know, I will be speaking to your mother. I met her at parent-teacher day and she seemed like the decent sort, so I expect she'll want to know exactly what has happened."

"My mother," said Jonah, "has cancer."

*

The class gasped audibly and Ross busied himself saying, "It's true," and, "She does," to those close enough to hear. Mitchell, who had gone behind his desk to write Jonah's hall pass, looked up with a face from which all the blood had suddenly drained.

"Mitchell, if you upset my mother, I swear to God I'll smash every window in your fucking house," Jonah said, his own voice ringing like a fire alarm within his head.

Jonah's mental clarity came from the kind of inner detachment that accompanies a full-scale mental breakdown; his logic was calm and brutal, his delivery terrifying. Pale and drawn, eyes ringed with dark fatigue, something deep inside of Jonah let go and rage spewed forth.

"So, yeah, go ahead and write my pass, dude. My mom's a little nervous about having her entire breast removed and could probably use two days to hang out with her son. But while you write that thing, you're going to listen to me. You don't know dick about what it means to be an adult. Man, if I were an adult, there's no fucking way I'd just sit here while some asshole made fun of my friend. I mean, when my friends asked me who I had for English this year and

I said, 'Mitchell,' everybody just groaned and made fun 'cause everybody knows that you're a dick and you're boring too. You can't teach me anything! What could you possibly know about being a grown-up if you can't even earn the respect of children! You don't even . . ."

Mitchell was writing the hall pass as fast as he could. Jonah continued careening wildly through his screed.

". . . and when I grow up, if my boss treats me like shit, I'm gonna find a new job. If I don't like my neighborhood, I'm gonna move. If I want to eat Cap'n Crunch for dinner every night, that's my business. This kid shit is for the birds. I didn't do my book report because I didn't have the fucking time!"

The rain crashed against the windows of the classroom and outside it was as dark as night.

"Why should I give a fuck if some old man can't catch a fish and then can't get home. It's not real! Hemingway made it up! When I'm grown up, I'm not going to have time for stuff like this. I'll have more important things to do. I'll have more interesting things to do. And I'll have the good sense to shave if I can't grow a real mustache!" Jonah, who'd stood up over the course of his tirade, slumped back down into his chair and rested.

*

With Mitchell's hall pass stuffed into his back pocket, Jonah walked slowly down the hall. In open defiance of Student Code Rule #45, he unwrapped a piece of gum and put it in his mouth, enjoying the rush of flavor. He wadded up the wrapper that read *"Crazy Grape"* in squiggly purple letters and positioned it between his thumb and middle finger.

"This doesn't taste a fucking thing like grapes," he said aloud, and flicked the wrapper toward one of the ghosts lining the walls on either side of the hallway.

*

Jonah marched like some existential Clint Eastwood toward the principal's office. Having beaten to death in front of his entire English class any hope he might have had for a normal school year,

Jonah now felt hard as rocks—an outlaw. Nothing would be the same. By teachers he would be hated and feared, by students he'd be revered as a hero, and both groups would give him the respect you'd give anyone who'd cut off his nose, not to spite his face, but because he prefers the look.

Jonah walked alone with his thoughts, while all around him the ghosts grew thicker, lining the hallway so the trail that Jonah followed became a thin path winding through a thicket of corpses. Obviously, he was about to be sent home, and this time he figured he'd treat his mom to the truth. The explanation was simple enough: Mitchell was being a dick and he decided to confront him. And then he lost his temper. Truth is nice that way, he thought. No scheming required. With Principal Liddy, he thought, discretion would have to be the better part of valor. A "yes sir" here, a "no sir" there, deny nothing, take your lumps, and get out of there. Of course, he'd have to find Liddy's office first. Jonah looked up from his musings to find that he was quite lost.

*

The ghosts were pressed in very closely on either side and Jonah could hear the hollow bones tinkling against one another like wind chimes. The path was so curvy now that Jonah couldn't see more than three or four feet ahead. He'd been walking now for what seemed like hours, but was still on the first floor. At least he thought he was; he didn't remember going up or down steps.

He stopped. "Where are you taking me?" he asked.

The question sounded as if he'd said it with his mouth jammed inside a drinking glass. Jonah paused, sensing trouble, but when he turned around, he found the way blocked. He turned back, but that was closed too. The bodies of the dead brushed against him as he struggled forward, sticking to his clothes like brambles.

Jonah dragged himself through the arms, elbows, and moist faces of the dead, fighting to keep the panic down.

*

His clothes hanging in tatters and his flesh scratched and stinging, Jonah pulled against hands that grabbed and pinched. A scream of revulsion and panic burst from his lungs, breaking the silence, and Jonah found himself stumbling into a clearing. He fell onto his hands and knees, gasping for breath. Ahead, he could see the door to the principal's office and, between him and it, the dead janitor.

Jonah turned to run, but the ghosts barred his way. Panic consumed him entirely. He spun around to face the janitor, tears filling his widened eyes, heart beating in his neck, searching for a way out and finding none. The janitor moved toward him, rolling up his sleeves, his motion fluid, graceful. Jonah's stomach seized and sent his breakfast blasting out through his mouth.

He looked infantile—coughing loudly from his diaphragm, puke dripping from his chin in stringy chunks—an image made complete when he evacuated spontaneously from both ends of his crotch.

"You, my young friend, are a mess," the janitor said, not without concern.

*

The janitor leaned in close, apparently undeterred by the array of smells that usually managed to stay unmixed and inside the body. He bent so that he could put his face right up to Jonah's. "My friends and I have a question for you." He straightened up, turned around, and walked a few steps with his palms together and his index fingers resting thoughtfully on his upper lip. After a moment, he turned back around: "WHAT THE FUCK ARE YOU DOING HERE?"

The sheer volume of the scream blinded Jonah. On the word "fuck," foam shot from the ghost's teeth, his face crimson and his eyeballs bulging. Jonah's legs buckled beneath him.

The janitor kneeled down in front of him and yelled again: "WHAT THE FUCK ARE YOU DOING HERE?"

Jonah sat with his legs splayed out and his elbows touching the ground in front of him. The janitor continued, "I'm going to beat you up now. But be forewarned. If you come back here again, I won't just beat you up. If you come back here again, I will beat you up and then I will fuck you."

He lifted Jonah by the hair into a standing position with one hand, while he drew back the other into a fist. As the fist came flying toward him, Jonah submerged, accessing dream time as he had so many times before. In that moment he found himself alone—safe and quiet. But the punch landed and knocked his lights out just the same.

*

When Jonah came to, he raised his eyelids on a very depressing scene: Prostrate in front of the principal's office, he was covered in urine, feces, vomit, saliva, and blood, dressed in tatters, and stupefied by the pain from what he was sure was a broken nose. Eager that no one see him like this, he began to move, only to find that his brain had been replaced with a bowling ball, the weight of which left him unable to lift his head. He squirmed onto his front, then onto his hands and knees, but that was as much as he could manage. He rolled onto his forehead searching for his nose, which he found, still under the skin, but just to the right of where it usually resided. Jonah tried to imagine what could possibly happen to make things worse.

When the bell rang.

*

The ringing of the bell clarified Jonah's thoughts: He could not allow himself to be seen like this. Gripping his head with both hands, he lifted himself in a clean-and-jerk motion, then wobbled into the main boys bathroom across from the principal's office. He managed to guide his momentum into the first stall that made itself available, then threw the lock, falling back against the pipes behind the bowl. The bathroom immediately became busy. With his head resting against the wall of the stall, Jonah allowed other people's conversation and the smell of urinal cakes to push thought from his mind.

*

The bell rang again and the bathroom slowly emptied, until it was just Jonah and the urinal cakes.

*

The second-period bell rang, and again the bathroom filled, with the echoing of voices and the sound of flushing. They have it so easy, Jonah thought to himself. The Carefree Happiness Club. Outside his box he could hear the sound of laughter and the tinkle of light, golden urine splashing happily into squeaky clean urinals. Inside, Jonah entertained vague feelings of hatred while tenderly exploring the new contours of his nose.

When the room emptied, Jonah continued to feel his nose, thinking about nothing.

*

He stepped out of his trousers and underwear, washed them in the toilet bowl, and then used the underwear as a washcloth to wipe the filth from his body, rinsing again and again until he felt he was as clean as he was going to get. Then he put his wet clothes back on and went to one of the sinks, where he used his shirt to clean his upper body and head. He had two black eyes and a broken nose.

*

He couldn't go to the doctor. Stomach pains could be caused by plenty of things, but there was no way a broken nose could be psychosomatic. He put his wallet between his teeth, grabbed his nose, and pulled as hard as he could, biting down against the pain until he felt the cartilage shift back into place. He then checked in the mirror to make sure it was straight, a difficult task as his vision was completely blurred by tears. It was without a doubt the most painful thing he'd ever experienced.

*

He walked home. What else was there to do? When he got there, he took four aspirin, which he chewed without tasting, stripped naked right there in the kitchen, threw his clothes in the trash, and went upstairs to sleep. After what he'd been through, he needed a nap.

*

Jonah opened his eyes, fighting sleep, looking for his dad. "Ah, forget it," he said to the room, sliding off the end of his bed and heading for the bathroom. The closer he got to the toilet, the harder it was to hold it, and halfway down the hall he started to run. He reached the door, touching the knob only long enough to free the latch, then pushed it open, bounding inside.

His father was on the toilet. Jonah screeched to a halt, backing up as his father immediately put his back to him, hiding whatever was on his lap. Jonah could have sworn a magazine flew up out of Dan's hands, but it turned into autumn leaves falling, obscuring Jonah's field of vision as his dad hurriedly pulled his trousers up over his skinny legs. Blackbirds flew out of nowhere, flapping noisily, and Jonah backed out of the room as fast as he could, unable to tear his eyes away. He crossed the threshold and slammed the door, leaning against it momentarily.

"Leave me *alone!*" he heard his father yell. "Leave me alone!"

Jonah pressed his face against the door and fell into a doze standing. The surface became slick and he realized he was crying.

*

Naked in his room, he wandered the hills and valleys of refuse, emptying his mind and touching familiar objects. He paused on the brink, deeply ready, beyond ready, over it already, so much so that when he lay spread-eagle on his bed, the water had already risen up around him. Jonah submerged, and the current came to take him away from the gleaming porcelain edge. In one short, violent motion, it grabbed him and sucked him in.

*

Facing down, Jonah could see for the first time that the placid layer he had likened to bathwater was really only the merest hovering of particles at the surface. The massive snaking and bubbling going on below churned beyond his ability to comprehend with a strength past imagining. He realized quite dispassionately that the magnitude of what he was seeing was bending his brain, and if he ever woke up, he just might have to live the rest of his life bent.

*

He was looking down through the universe, layer after layer after layer of diverging current, moving with geological momentum. One of the currents burst to the surface, bigger than anything he'd ever tried to imagine, but still just one small part of the writhing mass. Jonah was caught up in its wake. He rode on its broad back, over and down, and held his breath.

Three.

Two.

One.

Oblivion.

There are tiny spaces between currents, ribbons of equilibrium, made of things too small to be drawn up by the larger forces as they slither and slide against one another. This is where Jonah was. It was quiet and he rose slowly toward the surface, but the surrounding currents shifted and the ribbon was obliterated. How many times had this happened? Jonah couldn't be sure. The sensation was that of being punched over and over until the blows become only sound in the distance.

Within the dream, Jonah had a dream. He was at the beach and had drifted too far from the shore. His mother called to him, but he couldn't get to her. She couldn't see him, she could only call. As he would try to use one wave to get back in, another would crash down on him, carrying him back over and over again until Jonah lost himself entirely in the sound of the waves hissing in the distance.

FOURTH AND GOAL

JONAH OPENED HIS EYES but figured he was still dreaming because all he could see was his mother's face. Gradually he came to realize that she was touching him. He could feel one hand on his belly and the other stroking his forehead and it dawned on him that he wasn't dreaming anymore; he was awake. He smiled and drew in a deep breath of relief. Susan didn't smile back, still shocked and horrified by the welts and blisters that had risen spontaneously across Jonah's entire body. When Jonah finally noticed for himself, the pain came through all at once and he fainted.

*

His mother broke the silence.

"Jonah, we've got to talk. You've got to tell me what's going on."

She was right. But in his mind, he quickly sketched up the rough outline of a lie, details to be filled in as he went along. Then he looked his mom in the eye and began. Only nothing came out. The outline was only reflex; there was nothing behind it. Instead, he gently eased his battered body flat against the mattress and put first the pillow and then his forearm over his eyes. Thus relieved of the duties of interaction, he began. "I can see ghosts . . ."

*

He kept talking until he had told her everything. What he felt mostly was ashamed.

*

Jonah lay in the darkness beneath the pillow. When he felt his mother's hand on his foot, the contact sent a wave of relief through his body. For all he knew, she'd left midway through his tale to make arrangements to have him put away. He pulled himself up onto one elbow and took the pillow away from his face. It was wet with the tears that stung the cuts they happened into. "I'm sorry," he said.

"But you didn't do anything wrong."

"I know."

"So don't be sorry."

"Okay."

"Oh, Jonah . . ." Susan, suddenly mushy, pulled her son to her bosom, half of which would soon be leaving to join the other breasts lying in piles around the mammogram machine.

"Oh Jonah, what are we going to do?"

*

There was no "we" about it. Susan was going to have to make a decision. But the events she'd witnessed were so far beyond her understanding, and her son's calm explanations of what ghosts were and what they'd been doing to and around him for the last ten years were so utterly rational and reasoned, that when he was done, she found the decision already made. She believed her son. Which came as quite a relief.

"Hey, Jonah," she said, "want to get some ice cream?"

*

They decided to walk to the ice cream parlor, as Susan believed that walking stimulated thought. Even so, their discussion was going nowhere.

"Well, Jonah, we've got to talk to someone . . ."

"Like who?"

"Well, there's um . . ."

"Exactly."

"There's got to be somebody we can talk to. A medium or something."

They reached the ice cream store and Susan held the door for Jonah.

"Mom, could you get my ice cream while I wait out here?"

"Well, Jonah, I don't see why you—" Susan interrupted herself. "Is there a ghost in there?"

Jonah nodded. A dead guy standing by the register staring at the money, a dead woman slowly dancing to the reggae the teen employees had on the boom box, and three dead children with various grievous bodily injuries, all trying to lick the ice cream as it was scooped from tub to cone.

"Um, several," Jonah said, trying not to look.

"Ooh, where? Wait! Don't tell me . . ." Susan rushed into the store, looking about intently.

*

Susan returned with their ice cream, and they made their way to the small park across the street.

"It's no good; I couldn't see any."

"That's the way it works, Mom. No one else can see 'em."

Most of the benches were taken by winos snoozing in the warm, Indian summer evening, so they sat on the steps leading up to the statue occupying the center of the park.

"Why can't you just stop dreaming?"

Jonah thought about it. "What do you mean?"

"I mean, what if when the bathwater rises, you just don't go anywhere? Stay where you are?"

"I could do that."

"You don't sound convinced."

"It's not that. It's that . . ."

"What?"

"It's ghosts, Mom. I gotta get away from the ghosts. I think they're about to do something really bad."

"Spare change?" A homeless man appeared out of nowhere and Jonah screamed.

Susan put her arm around her son. "It's okay, Jonah. He's real."

*

After dinner, they talked some more.

"What are you going to do while I'm in the hospital?"

"Ross can come and stay."

Susan started to nip that one in the bud, then said, "You can't go back to school, can you?"

179

"Not unless you want to see me fucked in the ass by a ghost."

"Jonah!"

"But that's what he said he was going to do!"

"Are you sure he wasn't speaking figuratively?"

Jonah just looked at her.

"Okay, okay." Susan leaned back in her chair, bringing her herb tea with her. Since her diagnosis, their diet had gone from really good to immaculate. The shift to organic hadn't been tough; Jonah didn't even mind the seaweed and dietary algae that now appeared in everything they ate. But giving up coffee had been hard on both of them. Susan took a sip of her tea, then looked into the cup with obvious disappointment. "I'll be in the hospital for three days. I want you to think about it. Okay?"

"Okay."

"You know, I've been thinking."

Jonah looked up from his tea. "Yeah?"

"Well . . . maybe we should move."

"Really?"

"Sure. I mean, you've had nothing but bad luck since we moved here."

"What about your job?"

"It's not a job, Jonah, it's a skill. Besides, we've still got all your dad's stocks. And the insurance money from when he died. And our savings. Maybe I won't do anything for a while. Maybe I'll write a book."

"A book?"

"Sure. Why not?"

"About what?"

"Maybe I'll write a self-help book for single mothers whose kids can see ghosts."

*

Susan looked down at Jonah and Ross, squirming beneath her gaze, just short of giggles.

"Are you two sure you're going to be okay?"

All three of them knew it wasn't what she really meant. What she really meant was, *I'm about to go to the hospital. What assurances can you two maniacs give me that you're not going to burn my house to the ground?*

"Sure, Mom, we'll be fine."

"Yeah, Mrs. Hart, really."

Susan was not in the least bit reassured. When the doctor explained to her that the choice was really between losing the breast and dying, she characteristically embraced the circumstances she'd been forced into and began to busy herself with the details. She familiarized herself with the particulars of the procedure, learned that she might be in the hospital for as long as three days, and made arrangements with Mrs. Hand for Ross to stay with Jonah while she was gone. She contacted her insurance company, determined exactly what would be covered, and then consulted at length with her doctor's exasperated assistant to make sure there weren't any points of departure between her policy and their procedure. She contacted her bookseller and ordered several titles on the emotional aftereffects of the removal and reconstruction so she could learn what they might be and then avoid them. And one morning in the shower, she'd moved the washcloth along from face to neck to right arm to right breast to left arm to abdomen and realized that she had skipped the left breast entirely. This brought her immense satisfaction. A result, she felt, of thorough preparation.

"Okay. Um. Thursday's recycling day. Jonah, please don't forget to put the bins out by the curb. Oh, and don't turn the stereo up past four, the new tuner puts out more than the speakers can handle. Um, oh, one more thing, now I know you've gotten your range certification and I know there's no ammo in the house, but under no circumstances are you to handle the firearms. Am I making myself clear? Jonah? And that goes double for you, Ross. Now—"

"Mom."

"What?"

"Don't worry. Everything'll be fine."

"Well, yes. I know. But . . ."

"I'll be okay. Really."

Susan looked at him. She didn't want to go. Not because she was afraid to lose her breast. She was afraid to lose her son. She was afraid that when they cut her breast they might also cut some of the strings that attached her to her son and when she came back, he'd be gone. Jonah took her gently by the two fingers of her right hand and led her toward the cab that had just pulled up. "Come on, Mom, I'll walk with you."

Jonah accompanied his mother to her cab and gave her what he hoped was a reassuring hug. It lasted a while, and when it was done, he turned to go.

"Jonah, wait a minute."

"Yeah?"

Even though he was well out of earshot, Susan looked up to the porch to make sure Ross wasn't spying on them. He was lifting up his shirt and bending over to pick something out of his belly button. Susan returned her eyes to her son's.

"Are you going to be okay? If something happens to you while I'm gone, I'm never going to forgive myself."

"I don't know, Mom. Seems like just when I think I know what to expect, something different happens anyway. Who knows?"

"Maybe I shouldn't go."

Jonah just smiled.

"No, I know, you're right. But remember, you're the one who's got to decide where we go next. Even if it's just a hunch. When I'm out of the hospital, we're free to go. Anywhere. Okay?"

"Okay."

The wind picked up, sending fallen leaves skittering across the pavement. Above them, dark clouds blotted out the sun for a moment, then moved on. The morning was brisk, perfect sweater weather, and the air smelled like the leaves which were turning all around them.

"You called Mr. Segretti?" Jonah asked.

"Yeah. He agreed with your 'psychiatrist' that a 'month or so with your grandparents' would be 'just the thing.'"

They both smiled about this.

"Oh well," said Jonah, motioning up to the porch, "Dr. Hand is waiting."

Ross had found whatever it was he was looking for and held it up on his index finger for closer inspection.

"See you, Mom."

"See you, love."

*

Jonah decided to take his mother's advice. The plan was to go to sleep, but to just hang out in the lobby when he got there. He'd gotten so good at submerging that it took him the better part of that first night to remember how to just relax completely and have regular, though extremely vivid dreams. Eventually he found them, but they were disappointing, much like the herbal tea he'd been drinking. Still, on the occasions when he'd sink a little too deeply and feel the warm and wet begin to flow around him, he'd remember the alternative and slip back up into R.E.M. sleep.

It was no solution—in fact, it sucked. He was trapped, and when he and the man with the pitcher would look out the window in the second floor hallway, seeing the autumn wind blow the dead leaves around, he watched the hundreds of ghosts rolling along with the leaves with numb anxiety. He'd assured his mom that everything was fine and that nothing was going to happen to him, but that was just talk. The ghosts were coming for him. More of them every day. Soon they'd be strong enough to ignore the breeze. They'd just come right in and take him.

*

Ross came home from school and Jonah was waiting for him.

"How was school?"

"Sucked. Where's my piece?"

"On the TV."

"Thanks."

Ross went over to the TV and got the Glock. Jonah took the Peacemaker from his waistband and went to join his friend.

"Hey Jonah, you hungry?"

"Yeah. I already called the pizza guy."

"Alright! I'm so hungry, I . . ."

"Ross! Behind you!"

Both boys dove for cover, then blew huge, imaginary holes in whomever had challenged them. They'd decided to always be on the same side because even with the ammo locked away in the cabinet, looking down the barrel of a real gun made it somehow not so fun.

"Boom! Boom!"

"Sping! P-kew!"

"Eat lead, motherfucker!"

"Die! Die! Sp-ching!"

It was comfortable on the floor, and eventually the two boys fell to talking.

"Anything good happen at school?"

"Nah. Oh, Jimmy Thompson puked in the cafeteria."

"That's pretty good."

"Yeah, but I was hoping he'd start a chain reaction."

"Didn't?"

"Nah."

"Anybody ask about me?"

"Oh, yeah, everybody's talking."

"What'd they say?"

"Well, Jill Harper and all them are sure that you've been sent to the boys' farm. Mitchell came in Monday with a black eye and they all think you went to his house and beat him up."

"Cool!"

"Yeah, not bad. But Ben and Tom and those guys say you've been on tranquilizers for years and you freaked out because the guy at the drugstore fucked up on your prescription."

"Oh."

"Don't worry. If the rumor sucks, I totally deny it and make like I'm in a position to really know. But if it's good, I just get angry and go, 'Look, I told you, I can't say,' and they figure it must be true."

"Hey, thanks, man."

"*De nada.*"

Jonah looked at him, smiling, but Ross was suddenly serious.

"Jonah?"

"What?"

"I'm sorry about your mom."

"Thanks, Ross. She'll be alright."

"I know. But if . . ." Ross paused as one always does before the potentially objectionable, ". . . but if she's not . . . I mean, you know, if something happens, you can come stay with us. Live with us. I asked my mom. She said it was okay."

Jonah's heart broke with surplus love for his overweight friend.

*

The doorbell rang.

"The pizza guy!" they cried out in unison.

"Jonah! Cover me!"

Jonah complied and Ross ran on tiptoes up to the door, hiding the gun behind his back.

"Who's there?"

"Pizza."

"How can I be sure?" Ross shouted through the closed door.

"Fine, then. See ya."

"Wait!"

Ross opened the door partway and looked the delivery guy up and down.

"Okay, okay. Just set the pizza down."

"$14.50"

Ross turned his head back in.

"Jonah! Twenty!"

Jonah crawled on elbows and thighs to his mother's billfold, then, in similar fashion, brought the money to Ross.

"Okay. Now set the pizza down."

"Look, little dude, if you . . ."

"Do it and the twenty's yours."

"Whoa, okay."

The pizza guy took the twenty-dollar bill and trotted back to his car. After he pulled away, Ross slipped outside and inspected the pie.

"Relax, Jonah. It's pizza."

*

Technically, it was pizza. But when they brought it back to the television, cranked up MTV, and settled in for a feast, Jonah saw there were dead fingers all over it. They'd arranged themselves to spell out "*J-O-N-A-H.*"

*

The four of them—Jonah, Ross, and the two old dead ladies—sat on the sofa, heavily armed, eating, listening to the stereo, watching movies on the VCR, and returning fire anytime anyone on the screen started shooting. One of the old ladies had an air-cooled carbine; the other had a long-barreled hunting pistol with a scope. Jonah wondered if they could really shoot with those things. From time to time, he looked up to find one or both of them aiming their weapons at him.

"More chips?" Ross asked.

"Yeah, thanks." Jonah wiped his mouth on his hands. Their faces, covered in grease from the potato chips, gleamed in the pale light of the TV.

"Wanna see the car blow up again?" Jonah asked.

"Naw. Fast-forward to where her shirt comes off." Ross shifted and crossed his legs while Jonah obliged. They watched the scene roughly eighteen times.

"I'm getting another Coke," Jonah said. "Want one?"

"Yeah." Ross held his glass out without moving his eyes from the screen.

Jonah headed into the kitchen, weaving his way through the little dead girls who surrounded him, noticing that they too were armed. A few had small-caliber and novelty handguns, but most of them brandished harmless things—salt shakers, grapes, it was pathetic. Jonah watched them spar as he waited for the heads to settle on the two glasses of soda he'd poured. The old ladies could take these guys, no problem. He thought about that, staring at the drinks, his focus blurring and his mind wandering, not noticing his father as he approached and stood near as if to bring himself to Jonah's attention. Jonah stared off into space.

"Ahem." Dan cleared his throat.

"Oh!" Jonah started, sending the two glasses tumbling and the soda splashing across the counter. "Dad . . . shit!" Around him, the little dead girls sprang into action, jockeying for position to try to catch the Coke in their hands as it dripped from the counter's edge, and Jonah jumped back, out of their way. He looked up, about to yell at his father, when Ross interrupted.

"You okay?" he yelled from the next room.

"Yeah," Jonah called back. His dad looked different, but Jonah's irritation kept him from noticing how. "Yeah, I spilled the fucking Cokes."

"Oh. Could I have lemon in mine?"

Jonah looked at his father, but he could barely see him, or, rather, he could see right through him. He squinted, trying to see what he was doing, but it didn't help. Dan was fully dressed, with an overcoat and hat and what looked to be a pair of carry-on bags.

"Dad? Dad, I can't hear you."

"What?" yelled Ross.

"Nothing!" yelled Jonah, and then in a speaking voice repeated, "Nothing."

His dad was gone.

*

Back on the couch, the old lady next to him held the hunting pistol. Smiling, she placed it to his temple and Jonah could feel the barrel, cold and hard against his skin. Jonah returned his attention to the movie and wondered if he was going to die now.

*

The two boys took their shirts off. After all, the men who were on-screen and lost in the jungles of Southeast Asia had. Only when they did that, the old ladies took their dresses off. It didn't bother Ross, who was as oblivious to ghosts as he was to everything else, but it had Jonah squirming.

"Hey, Jonah, do you think that . . . Oh, no way!"

"What?"

"What do you mean, 'What?' Point-blank range and he missed. An old lady could have hit him!"

Jonah didn't doubt it. The old ladies gave each other high-fives over the boys' heads and the sound made Jonah flinch. Since they'd stripped down to their slips, the room smelled like fried food.

"Hey, Jonah, do you believe in ghosts?"

You could have knocked Jonah over with a pin. "Um, yeah, I do."

"If I tell you something, do you promise not to tell anyone?"

"Ross, when have I ever . . ."

"Dude, just promise me, okay?"

"Okay. I promise."

Ross looked at him warily, then spoke. "I've seen some."

*

The two old ladies moved in on either side of Ross, and each cupped a hand to her ear to better catch what he said.

187

"Really?"

"Really. Or I think so, anyway. You know the abandoned house behind the supermarket?"

Jonah did. The place was definitely haunted. Originally built as a summer home, it had fallen into the possession of the owner's three sons, none of whom ever married. They'd watched resentfully as the city had grown to surround them, their hatred intensified by the necessity of selling off parcels of their land to developers in order to make ends meet. They lived well into their eighties and had died in the order that they were born, one with cancer of the lip, the next with cirrhosis, and the last from a heart attack, brought on when his cigarette dropped from his mouth and set his pajamas on fire as he sat on the porch glaring at children on their way to school. Now all three sat on the porch glaring, but since the road in front of their house had been rerouted, visitors were few and far between. Mostly, they glared at the trees that choked the lot. Or at anyone who wanted to brave the tangled shortcut to the supermarket.

"So anyway, my mom sent me to the store to get some food coloring, and I took the shortcut. As I came around the corner by that old car, I could have sworn that I saw three guys sitting on the porch. But when I really looked, no one was there. Weird or what?"

Jonah nodded but said nothing. He could feel the barrels of the two guns scraping the sides of his head as he moved it up and down.

"Jonah! Down!" Ross yelled. Jonah tried to comply but found his head trapped between the two guns, held as if in a vice. Ross flung himself to the ground and pretended to return fire.

"Boom!" Ross yelled.

Jonah lost it. "Do it!" he yelled, trying with all his might to turn to either side, but finding it impossible. "Just do it! I don't fucking care!"

"Boom!" yelled Ross.

"Do it! Just fucking do it! Shoot me or go away!" Hatred and anger boiled over and Jonah swung wildly to either side, trying to strike the old ladies.

"I hate you, I hate you, I hate you . . ."

Boom.

*

Jonah stared across a vast expanse of white, limitless and without perspective.

"Dad?"

"Yes?"

"Am I dead?"

"No, son. Ross shot the TV."

Jonah looked down and saw himself unconscious on the sofa and the TV on its back, smoke rising from the hole in the screen. Ross paced back and forth pulling his hair and crying. Viewing the scene, he became aware of a slight ringing sound, far away. He looked back up and saw the bright whiteness beginning to diminish.

"Dad!"

"Yes, son?"

"Don't go."

The pure, white light continued to dissipate, like water soaking into a sponge. His father's voice was close, all around him, but increasingly faint.

"Goodbye."

"Dad! Don't die! Dad, please don't die."

Jonah watched as the light withdrew into a point, flickered, then disappeared.

*

Jonah opened his eyes, looked out from his body, and found himself crying. "My dad's dead," he said, but all he could hear was the ringing in his ears.

And then Ross was on him, crying and slobbering, "Ohmygodohmygod, Jonah, I'm so sorry, I loaded it, but I unloaded it. Shitshitshitshit, I'msorryi'msorryi'msorry, I didn't mean to . . ."

"You put the clip in?" Jonah asked, his voice now slightly audible above the ringing.

"But I took it out! I took it out I took it out!"

"You left a bullet in the chamber."

"Jonah, I'm sorry, I'm sooooooooooooo sorry . . ." Ross flung himself back up and returned to pacing and pulling his hair. Jonah smiled despite the tears streaming down his face.

The dead ladies! Jonah remembered and rose with a start, turning to face the sofa. It was empty.

*

Jonah ran from the kitchen to the top of the stairs, in and out of the bathroom, and finally to the window at the front of the house. They were gone. The two old dead ladies, the little dead girls, the lady in the sink, and the man with the pitcher were gone.

*

DOWNWARD DOG

"HAVE ANOTHER, MR. HART?"

Dan tapped the base of his empty martini glass, weighing his options. "One more, Kirby, one more—make it with three olives, though." Dan flashed his smile. "It's supposed to be lunch."

"No meetings this afternoon, I take it?" said the bartender, shaking the martini and laughing.

"A birthday party," Dan corrected. "My little man turns six today. Ahh, thanks . . ."

Dan took the drink, sipped it twice, then set it down and watched the gin and vermouth gently roil against one another.

"I got one too, turned six in the spring. Took him to an Orioles game, eyes like saucers the whole time. Taking yours anywhere?"

"Not sure. His mother arranges things like that." Dan drained half his glass, unconsciously embracing the stinging in his throat. "Speaking of which . . ." he said, sliding from his stool and reaching into his pocket for his keys, ". . . *A domani.*"

"See you tomorrow, Mr. Hart."

*

Dan turned the key in the ignition and felt his car, a Porsche 911 Carrera Coupé, leap into life. Gliding easily between the cement posts of the underground parking garage, he steered toward the attendant's booth and fished in the glove compartment for a cassette.

"Here it . . . no . . ."

He paid the man in the booth without looking at him and returned his hand to the wheel. He paused at the sidewalk at the top of the ramp and pulled out into traffic.

Dan drew a cassette from the glove compartment and scanned the label on either side, then threw it to the floor. Reaching for another, he returned his eyes to the road just in time to see the cars stopped at the red light ahead of him. When he slammed down on the brakes, the Porsche's wheels locked into a skid, which brought him up short, inches from the car in front of him.

"Fuck!"

When the light turned green and the cars ahead of him pulled away, Dan followed, heart still racing in his chest. "Okay, steady as she goes," he said, shaking his head in an attempt to clear it. "Deep breaths, deeeeeeeep breaths . . ."

*

Cruising the parkway, Dan leaned into the turn as he accelerated. *"Changes in latitude, changes in attitude . . ."* he sang. "Where is that fucking thing?" He rummaged anew in the glove compartment, flinging cassette after cassette to the floor. "No . . . no . . . no . . . Aha!"

Dan looked up just as his car left the road and shot up the embankment. With the abrupt change in trajectory, his nose hit the steering wheel, knocking him unconscious. Clearing the ridge, Dan floated momentarily in his beloved Porsche until it touched earth, first with the right side, then with its left—then down into the gully, where he passed through the windshield and came to rest, a pile of moist red ribbons, in the leaves at the bottom.

*

Dan awoke, as if from sleep, his dreams still clinging to him: conversations with his son, weird ones in which his words had no sound and his son was older. Was I that drunk? I don't even remember the birthday party. A fragment of the last dream rose within his mind, Jonah crying and screaming, *"Don't Die!"* Dan's heart froze within his chest. He could see it all: every clever rejoinder, each sleek possession, each hallowed drink—it was nothing! Oh my God, he thought, I've failed—I've failed utterly!

"Jonah!" Dan screamed, but there was no sound. Shame and grief gripped him and he sobbed, bodiless. I never really lived. Jonah— Susan!—I'm sorry . . .

Warm arms of light encircled him and Dan felt his edges blur. Goodbye, he thought. Good night.

Also from AKASHIC BOOKS

THE NAMES OF RIVERS by Daniel Buckman
197 pages, hardcover; $21.00, ISBN: 1-888451-29-7
"Let the word go out: There's a new Hemingway loose in America. Buckman's powers of observation are breathtaking, his lyricism continually puts a fresh face on the mundane things that usually pass unnoticed, and his prose rolls forward with a sure rhythm, concision and grace that make almost every paragraph a textbook model of how to write well."
　　　　　　　　　　　　　　　　　—*San Francisco Chronicle*

THE ICE-CREAM HEADACHE by James Jones
235 pages, trade paperback; $13.95, ISBN: 1-888451-35-1
"The thirteen stories are anything but dated . . . a compact social history of what it was like for Mr. Jones's generation to grow up, go to war, marry, and generally, to become people in America."
　　　　　　　　　　　　　　　　　　　　　—*The Nation*

SEED by Mustafa Mutabaruka
*Selected for the *WASHINGTON POST'S* Best Novels of 2002 list.*
*Selected for *LIBRARY JOURNAL'S* Best First Novels of Spring/Summer 2002 list.*
178 pages, trade paperback; $14.95, ISBN: 1-888451-31-9
"Mutabaruka's deft maneuvering between past and present, Morocco and the United States, blurs distinctions and creates a mystical and frightening story . . . [P]lain prose and interesting characters keep this novel on its feet and make it dance."
　　　　　　　　　　　　　　　　　　　—*Library Journal*

SUICIDE CASANOVA by Arthur Nersesian
370 pages, hardcover binding into hard-plastic videocassette;
$25.00, ISBN: 1-888451-30-0
"Sick, depraved, and heartbreaking—in other words, a great read, a great book. *Suicide Casanova* is erotic noir and Nersesian's hard-boiled prose comes at you like a jailhouse confession."
　　　　　　　　　　　—Jonathan Ames, author of *The Extra Man*